LC

FRIENDS
OF AC

D0106243

Tales of J

AUG 2 1 2008

Tales of Juha

CLASSIC ARAB FOLK HUMOR

edited by Salma Khadra Jayyusi
translated by Matthew Sorenson,
Faisal Khadra, and Christopher Tingley
introduction by Said Yaqtine

Interlink Books

An imprint of Interlink Publishing Group, Inc.
Northampton, Massachusetts

To Yasmeen Qaddumi
from her loving parents Nabil and Huda,
who shared with her a love for Juha

First published in 2007 by

INTERLINK BOOKS
An imprint of Interlink Publishing Group, Inc.
46 Crosby Street, Northampton, Massachusetts 01060
www.interlinkbooks.com

Translation copyright © by Salma Khadra Jayyusi, 2007

All rights reserved. No part of this publication may be reproduced,
stored in a retrieval system, or transmitted in any form or by any
means, electronic, mechanical, photocopying, recording or otherwise
without the prior permission of the publisher.

Library of Congress Cataloging-in-Publication Data
Tales of Juha : classic Arab folk humor / edited by Salma Khadra
Jayyusi ; translated by Matthew Sorenson, Faisal Khadra, and
Christopher Tingley ; introduction by Said Yaqtine.
p. cm.
ISBN 1-56656-641-X   ISBN 13: 978-1-56656-641-4
1. Nasreddin Hoca (Legendary character) 2. Arabic wit and humor—
Translations into English. I. Jayyusi, Salma Khadra. II. Sorenson,
Matthew R. III. Khadra, Faisal. IV. Tingley, Christopher.
PN6231.N27T25 2006
892.7'70080351—dc22
2006015059

This English translation is published with the cooperation of PROTA,
(the Project of Translation from Arabic); director: Salma K. Jayyusi,
Cambridge, Massachusetts, USA.

Printed and bound in the United States of America

To request our complete 40-page full-color catalog,
please call us toll free at **1-800-238-LINK,** visit our
website at **www.interlinkbooks.com**, or write to
Interlink Publishing
46 Crosby Street, Northampton, MA 01060
e-mail: info@interlinkbooks.com

Contents

Acknowledgments

On a visit to Kuwait, staying with my friend Dr. Ghada Qaddumi, I once again enjoyed the warmth and hospitality of the Qaddumis, reminding me of old days in Kuwait in the 1960s, when all of us lived there. One afternoon, Ghada's family gathered around us, and Yasmeen, Ghada's lovely granddaughter, then only eight, asked if I would like to hear some anecdotes from Juha. She then, with the visible pleasure only a child can fully show, read to us some of the more famous Juha anecdotes. So absorbed was she in the reading, so clearly enthralled, that I felt deeply touched by the recurring scene of an Arab child's early initiation into this timeless, ever alive personality. Yasmeen's parents seemed to share my feelings, and her father Nabil, whom I had known as a child with far-reaching dreams and was now a successful business-man, asked if I would like to include, in my PROTA program, a book of Juha anecdotes, which he would happily support and dedicate to Yasmeen.

This was a welcome invitation, as all the books we had done previously were far from jocular litera-ture, reflecting a contemporary Arab world hardly involved with the merry side of life. I am now happy to offer this book to English speakers, adults and children alike. Jocular literature is universal, and, for all the genuine differences among various cultures regarding particular taste, there are certain comic personalities that cross the boundaries with ease and weave their way into a different culture. I think Juha is one such personality.

I want here to thank, first and foremost, Nabil Qaddumi and his wife Huda for their care and generosity in spontaneously suggesting and subsidizing the translation of this work—the first PROTA publication to have been suggested personally by the donors themselves. I should also like to thank Professor Ulrich Marzolf of Göttingen University, for the consultation he kindly provided regarding Juha and his work. Many thanks go to Said Yaqtine, an eminent specialist on Arab jocular literature, for agreeing to write the cogent introduction to this book at short notice. Many thanks and much appreciation go to Matthew Sorenson, my student during my happy University of Utah days and a true lover of literature, for his initial translation of the texts from Arabic. Many heartfelt thanks go, too, to Christopher Tingley, not only for the excellent work he did on the text as co-translator but also for the joy he shared with me over the work and for his constant reminders, by bringing forward similar anecdotes from European popular culture, of the universality of Juha's anecdotes. I am also most grateful to my brother Faisal Khadra's labor of love on the initial translated work. His natural sense of humor helped us greatly in sustaining Juha's appeal by tapping into the stores of laughter within us.

—*Salma Khadra Jayyusi*
Director, East–West Nexus/PROTA
Boston–London–Jordan

The Unforgettable Juha
by Said Yaqtine

I remember how, when I was young, the book *The Chief Anecdotes of Juha* (*nawadir Juha al-kubra*) was offered for sale on the pavements of public squares, side by side with books about the interpretation of dreams, *The Fragrant Orchard* (*al-rawd al-'aatir*), al-Manfaluti's and Gibran's texts, and the tales of *Samira, Daughter of the Arabian Peninsula*. The special status enjoyed by the book, along with those named and others like them, made Juha accessible at all times; whenever the available batch was sold out, another would be produced. Each one of us would buy or rent a copy, to snatch a moment of laughter or store the anecdotes in the memory, so as to recount them to the satisfaction and pleasure of those who heard them. The name of Juha, so light and simple, would come up regularly, and we would have fun passing around the stories about him. We might even attach his name to some of those among us, as a way of describing particular kinds of behavior, or an odd role someone had assumed.

If Juha's character maintains this kind of presence in the world of the young, so it does equally for adults. Juha is a personality that grows along with each of us, ever present in the memory; and, at many points in our lives, we find ourselves recalling what we have read or heard about it. We find this personality, as expressed in sayings and deeds, a beguiling one, one that makes the world of laughter constantly accessible through its characteristic features of entertainment and irony.

Books from the Arab-Islamic heritage are full of characters rivaling Juha with their special worlds and innocent magic, able, like him, to set a smile on the face: characters such as Abu Dulama, Ash'ab the greedy, Ibn al-Jassas, Habannaqa, and the characters in al-Jahiz's *Misers* (*al-bukhala'*). These books are replete, too, with a wealth of characters living in their distinctive worlds: brocade vendors, jesters, idiots, simpletons, thieves, vagabonds, afflicted people, the thin-haired, and so on. The characters have various common features, foremost among which is their capacity to provoke laughter and sarcasm at the expense of others. All, though, fade before Juha's over-whelming presence; his portrayal emerges, in relief, as wider and more comprehensively typical than ever.

If all these other characters, and the worlds they represent, have remained within a written dimension, faithfully tied to the sources that have passed down anecdotes about them, Juha's character has broken out from the world of the book into that of daily intercourse. As such, it has infiltrated all classes and milieus, and has crossed the various dialects used within the Arab and Islamic worlds. Indeed, it has even migrated—in much the same way as great motifs do—to a number of other countries and languages. In all these contexts, anecdotes of Juha are recounted orally, and they may also be included in the innovative texts of playwrights, novelists, and painters.[1] Such anecdotes are frequently reprinted in various forms, and, when we finally sail off into the networks of cyberspace, it is surprising to see how many sites bear the name "Juha" and present his deeds and sayings.

What is it that has endowed this character with such a presence and such an influence as to transcend time and float in space? To be ever present by virtue of deeds so unlike ordinary deeds, and utterances so far removed from the commonplace?

Juha: A World of Multidimensional Signs

It is fruitful to go back to historical and literary sources, and to chart what has been said of Juha; by doing this, we may hope to form a comprehensive portrait of the character. And yet, the numerous, disparate viewpoints on Juha's personality only make it clearer than ever that the particularity of Juha lies not in any mere factual basis, but rather in what the anecdotes woven around this character can give us.

Different sources provide us with various clear-cut identities[2]. He was, we are told, Abu 'l-Ghusn Dujain bin Thabit of the Fazara tribe who lived in the fourth century AH (tenth century CE). Anecdotes about him were transmitted to Turkey and attributed thereafter to a further person. At other times he is named as al-Khoja Nasruddin al-Rumi, who was born in 605/1208 and died in 683/1284 in a village in Anatolia. Various further identities attach to Juha: some say his name was Nuh (Noah), another gives him the name Dujain bin Thabit or al-Dujain bin al-Harith, while still another calls him Abdullah. As for foreign languages, Abdul Sattar Farraj notes that his name in Italian is

"Giucca" or "Giova,"[3] and that the Maltese form is "Jahan." We find differences not only as to name but in chronological setting. He is placed as a contemporary of Abu Muslim al-Khurasani (second/ eighth century), or of Genghis Khan (thirteenth century CE), or of Tamerlane (fourteenth century CE).

Differences also attach to the material recounted. Some of it we find linked to the fables of Aesop, or else derived from tales of the Arab heritage, with the character's name changed to attribute them to Juha. Specific parts may be closely identified with elements in *Kalila and Dimna* (*Kalila wa Dimna*), as with the story recounted by Kalila to Dimna about a merchant who goes on a journey after leaving some iron with a friend. On his return, he is told rats have eaten up the iron. The merchant accordingly hides his friend's child, and, when asked if he has seen him, relates how he saw a hawk carrying off a child. An almost identical story is found among the anecdotes of Juha. Then again, we find a story of how thieves enter Juha's house while he is asleep with his wife; this motif is set, with various endings, within some of the stories of Kalila and Dimna.

The multiplicity of characters and tales cross-referencing with Juha compels us to inquire as to the "reality" of the Juha character itself. Does every era, every period and locality, have its Juha? In fact, the presumed "true" or "factual" Juha has been transposed from his historical character to that of a stock figure, an iconized character, a symbol. He has become the representative of the type, and is both object and interpreter. We are faced with a world of signs, each consistent with the other and deriving from the other, often multisided in its meaning.

Juha embodies, then, a world of multiple signs; and, as such, he crosses over from being an imaginary "character" to become a human being of every place and time. This is why he remains so vividly present, even ingrained, in the memory. He cannot be forgotten because he sums up, in himself, a complex, intricate human universe that endures through time and is unaffected by change of place.

Juha: The Balance of Opposites

What distinguishes Juha from other, similar characters in the literary heritage (many of them with their own depth and human dimension) is his transformation to become the focus of a popular narrative capable of expansion and of constant amendment and editing. From the ever-changing real world, actual events can be adopted and attributed to him, just so long as they cause embarrassment to the real-life characters in question or further an artistic aim. Moreover, part of his own universe, derived from what is recounted of him, can be transformed and attributed to someone else—though even then we find, when we examine closely and turn to sources, that it continues to reflect him.

Juha has become the fount of an inventiveness that is prolific and ongoing—a reflection of the qualities, notably complex, articulate and rich, that are to be found in his own character. These qualities, taken together, constitute an ambivalent character, one embodying a balance of opposites.

When we examine Juha's world of storytelling, we find it to be universally appropriate, regardless of individual age and experience. Various types of character are represented, and, in the process, various portrayals emerge, many of them contradictory.

He appears in the following roles: shepherd, judge, merchant, scholar, saint, thief, and so on. More generally, he appears as wealthy man or pauper, generous man or miser, intelligent man or simpleton, bachelor or married man. It is a world of different features and numerous contradictory aspects, representing humanity in all its variety of category, status, and individual personality.

This multidimensional character has its basis and its prop. The basis is the balance of opposites, and the prop is paradox.

The balance of opposites appears at the level of actions or events, through a non-stock character which, in its multiplicity, reflects the conflict between strength and weakness, between authority and submission. Through the anecdotes, Juha's character is manifest in this conflict. It champions "eccentric" logic because this is different from prevailing logic; its "idiocy" sets up an authority in opposition to authoritatively predominant "reason"; and its "wit" triumphs over rationalizing "idiocy." In this lies the distinctiveness of Juha's character: he is the wisest yet the most simple-minded of people.

The balance of opposites is likewise conveyed to us at the level of his own spoken language, or through the language in which the anecdotes about him are expressed. The basis in paradox is clear from the purely denotative nature of Juha's language, void as it is of intimation and metaphor. Language here reverts to its primary mode, without the many suggestive elements that might be present in the various contexts within which that language is employed. As such, Juha's anecdotes achieve their dimension of paradox by means of the language in use among people.

In addition to reliance on a "literal" language, we find, on the level of meaning, a reduction to things at their most primary. There is no logic, no drawing out of meaning through analogy: everything becomes inverted, taking on a meaning that runs counter to the norms of common sense and conventional pattern. This is why Juha's actions and sayings stimulate us and make us laugh. His world becomes a living paradox vis-à-vis the ordinary world of people; and yet, at the same time, it is the best and most profound expression of their world and their feelings.

Juha is the representation of the Arab imagination in all eras. So it is that his anecdotes force us to view ourselves in the mirror of his world (that of laughter), while drawing us, at the same time, toward an ironical view of ourselves. He is visible in daily life with all its joys and miseries, and in its characteristic values or defeats. The anecdote, centered on Juha's own "self," develops to represent a position of "compromise," at once self-critical (individually and collectively) and focalized through an artistic mirror.

That is why we cannot forget Juha.

Notes

1 'Ali Ahmad Bakthir has written a play called *Juha's Nail* (*mismar Juha*); Nabil Badran has written another, *Juha Sold His Donkey, a Comedy in Three Acts* (*Juha ba'a himarah, masrahiyya fi thalathat fusul*) (Damascus: Union of Writers, 1980); 'Abd al-Fattah Rawwas Qal'aji followed suit with a play entitled, *A City of Straw* (*madina min qash*), which can be found at www.musraheon.com site. The Moroccan theater of the 1970s witnessed a surge of short plays about Juha, while the Algerian writer Kateb Yacine made Juha the subject of his play *Mohammed, Pack Your Case and Go* (*Mohammed prends ta valise*) (Paris: edi. Seuil, Paris, 1999). In his novel *Sunstroke* (*L'insolation*) (Paris: Gallimard, 1987), Rashid Bujadra made Juha a revolutionary hero. There are, moreover, many publications geared to children, containing anecdotes of Juha with accompanying drawings. For a single example, see Mustafa 'Ali, ed., *Laugh with Juha: Fifty and One Anecdotes* (Cairo: Maktabat al-Qur'an, 2000.)

2 Of the numerous studies, we may mention here: *The Anecdotes of Juha* (*akhbar Juha*), researched and edited by 'Abd al-Sattar Ahmad Farraj (Cairo: Library of Egypt, 2nd edition, n.d.) and *The Arabic Juha* (*Juha al-'Arabi*) by Muhammad Rajab al-Najjar (Kuwait: 'Alam al-Ma'rifa Series, No. 10, October 1978).

3 According to Jean Déjeux, his name among the Sicilians is "Giufà." See his important article "Sous le signe de Djoh'a," in *Autrement, L'Humour*, No. 131, September 1992.

. 1 .

Wit and Wisdom

A merchant went into a restaurant and ordered a chicken and two eggs. He would, he said, pay the restaurant owner in three months' time, when he came back from a business trip. On his return he went to the restaurant and asked to settle the bill in full.

"The account's a high one," the restaurant owner said, "but I'll settle for two hundred dirhams."

"In heaven's name," the merchant cried, "how could you ask two hundred dirhams, even for two chickens and four eggs?"

"Well," explained the restaurant owner, "if the chicken you ate three months ago had still been alive, and laid one egg a day to be put under a hen, we would have had so many chickens and so many eggs. We could have sold them for hundreds of dirhams."

After a heated argument, they ended up at the court of a judge who was in collusion with the restaurant owner. The judge asked the merchant if he'd agreed the price with the restaurant owner three months before, and the merchant said he hadn't. And, pursued the judge, might the chicken and the two eggs not have produced hundreds of eggs and chickens in the meantime?

"Of course they might," said the merchant, "if the chicken had still been alive. But it had been killed and roasted, and the two eggs had been fried."

The judge seemed inclined, even so, to rule against the merchant. And so the merchant asked for a postponement until the next day, when he'd have further evidence to submit. The judge agreed to this.

Next morning the merchant arrived and stated that Juha would be submitting the proof of his case. They waited, but Juha was very late. At last he turned up.

"Why have you been so long?" the judge shouted furiously. "Keeping us waiting like this?"

"Don't be angry, sir," Juha replied meekly. "I was just about to come when my partner, in some land we're going to plant with wheat, came and asked for the seed. So I waited until I'd boiled around two big sacks full of wheat, then I gave them to him to sow. That's why I'm late."

"An odd sort of excuse that is!" the judge said sarcastically. "Whoever heard of wheat being boiled before it's sown?"

"And," said Juha at once, "whoever heard of a roasted chicken and fried eggs reproducing and multiplying so much that they're worth the two hundred dirhams this merchant's claiming?"

The judge, taken aback, ruled in favor of the merchant.

⁕⁂⁕

When Juha was a judge, two voluptuously charming women approached him.

"I placed an order with this woman," one of them said, "to make me some thick thread. Instead, she made the thread thin. Make her give me back my money."

With that she unveiled a face as lovely as a full moon, and showed her glittering hair the color of gold bars.

"Praise be to God!" Juha said. Then he looked at the second woman. "What do you have to say?" he asked her.

"Our agreement," she replied, her voice shaking with anger, "was that the thread should be like this little finger of mine, not like my arm." And with that she revealed an arm with the thickness of a rod of silver or crystal.

"Enough, daughter, enough," Juha told her. "Don't make the thread so thick it will burst, or so thin it will waste, like the heart of your shaikh Juha!"

❦

Juha used to preach to those who attended his council about the futility of life and how foolish men were sometimes; about man's narrow horizons, and his constant, ceaseless searching after passing material things, and all the wars and hatreds such a search led to.

"And what, after all," Juha would ask, "does man take with him at last, when he dies?"

"Nothing," they'd all answer.

"And this 'nothing,'" Juha would tell them then, "is the hard, high price people don't gain until it's too late."

❦

Juha was walking on the outskirts of the city with a big bag of money, when he found his way barred by two thieves, each wielding a large knife. They threatened to kill him unless he handed the bag over to them.

"Just give me a moment," he said, "to calm down, after the fright you've given me." And he told them to sit down, so they could sort the matter out between them. So, the three sat down on the ground.

"I've a good deal of money," Juha told them, "but I'll only give it to one of you. So, agree between yourselves which one's going to have it."

The first thief said he had sole right to the money, because he was the one who'd caught sight of Juha on the road. The second thief said, no, he should have the money, as he was the one who'd noticed the bag. Juha addressed the two of them.

"There's no need for disagreement," he said. "It'll only end in regrets. Talk it over between yourselves and come to a peaceable agreement about who's entitled to the money."

But the two thieves couldn't agree, and the dispute grew bitter, though it remained confined to words.

"I've had a bright idea," Juha told them then. "I'll give the money to whichever of you's the stronger."

"I'm stronger than my comrade," the first thief asserted. "And I'll break his head for him!"

"I'm the stronger one," retorted the second thief. "I'll kill my comrade with a single blow!"

Taking advantage of the dispute, Juha addressed the two of them.

"Now," he said, "both of you, make good on what you've said."

The thieves came to violent blows. Each broke the other's head, and they fell bleeding to the ground. When Juha had made sure they couldn't get up, he left them and fled.

One night, while Juha and his wife were in bed, he heard footsteps up on the roof. He woke his wife and whispered in her ear to pretend to wake him, then ask him how he'd amassed all his wealth. This she did.

"When I was young," he told her, "I used to rob houses. And whenever I climbed up onto the roof of a house, I'd wait until the moon rose and its beams were shining down on the skylight. Then I'd grab the rays, say *shawlam, shawlam*, seven times, and slide down on the beams, into the house. I didn't need a rope. Once I was finished, I'd climb back up the same way. No one in the house had any idea I was there."

The thief, hearing this, decided he'd picked up a tip that night that was even more precious than anything he might be able to steal. He waited for the moon to rise. Then, when the beams were going down into the skylight, he said, *shawlam, shawlam*, seven times, and grabbed at the beams to let himself down through. He fell to the floor and broke his ribs; whereupon Juha rushed over to him, telling his wife to light the lamp before he could escape. But the thief told him: "Don't have any fears, brother. As long as you're so greatly, wondrously wise, and I'm so stupid, I won't escape you so easily."

*

Juha went for a swim in the river, undressing and leaving his clothes on the bank. Some thief or other stole them, and Juha had to go home completely naked. A few days later, he went to the river and took a dip fully clothed. His friends, seeing him, asked him what he thought he was doing.

"Better for my clothes to get wet on me," he answered, "than be dry on someone else!"

⁕⁂⁕

Juha's donkey was stolen, and his friends came around to see him.

"It's your own fault," one of them said. "You should have been more careful and locked the gate to your house."

"The wall to the house must be far too low," said a second. "It's all your own fault."

"You must have committed some kind of wrong," said a third, "and the Almighty's punished you by letting your donkey be stolen."

"You must be pretty stupid," a fourth friend commented, "letting a thief steal your donkey, and you didn't even notice."

"I locked the gate to the house," Juha retorted, "the wall's a high one, and I took every precaution. You're blaming me. Isn't it the thief who should get the blame? Or do you maybe think he isn't to blame at all?"

⁕⁂⁕

Juha had a large number of iron rods stored up, and, since he was going on a long and distant journey, he left these with a neighbor for safe keeping. When he returned, he went to the neighbor to claim them back.

"I'm so sorry, friend," the neighbor told him. "I'm plagued with mice, and they've eaten your iron rods."

"Have a fear of God, my good shaikh!" Juha retorted. "How can mice eat iron?"

"Well, that's what happened," the neighbor said. "If you don't believe me, let's go to the warehouse, and you'll see for yourself."

Juha pondered the matter carefully.

"You're telling the truth, I'm sure," he said at last, sarcastically. "No one can deny mice eat iron, just the way they do butter, sugar and bread—at least when the iron's in your house. I leave matters to God's will."

A few days after this, Juha followed one of his neighbor's young children, then took him to his own house and hid him there. The merchant neighbor, unable to find his son, became frantic. Next day Juha went to his neighbor's house.

"I'm sorry, friend," he said, "about your son's disappearance. And I'm sorrier still he won't be coming back to you."

"How do you know that?" the merchant cried.

"I saw a bird," Juha replied, "seize your son and carry him off."

The merchant shook Juha by the shoulder.

"A bird," he said, "seizing a little child? Fear God, shaikh Juha. Don't say such things!"

Juha smiled. "You too, shaikh," he said, "should have a fear of God, and not say such things."

"What did I say?" the merchant demanded.

"You told me," Juha answered, "that mice had eaten my iron rods."

The neighbor realized then that it was Juha who'd abducted his son, in retaliation for his denial about the iron rods. He led Juha to a large underground warehouse.

"You're a sly old bird yourself!" he told him. "Take your iron rods and give me back my son!"

*

It happened that Juha stole a donkey and took it to the market to sell—then lost it in turn to another thief.

"How much did you sell the donkey for?" someone asked him later.

"At cost," Juha replied.

*

Juha went with a man on a trip. When they were having a rest, the man asked Juha to go and buy some meat, but Juha said he couldn't; so, the man went and bought the meat himself. Then he asked Juha to cook it, but Juha said he didn't know how to cook; so, the man cooked the meat. Then he asked Juha to make bread crumbs to add to the meat, but Juha said he didn't feel like it; so, the man prepared them. Then he asked Juha to stir the meat and bread in the pot, but Juha said he was afraid the pot would be upset and spoil his clothes; so, the man did the stirring. Finally the man told Juha: "Come and eat."

"By God," Juha said, "I feel so ashamed now, that I turned down all your requests before."

And with that he got up and ate.

*

One day Juha was asked how old he was, and he answered that he was forty. Ten years later they asked him again, and again he answered that he was forty.

"Ten years ago," they said, "we asked you how old you were, and you said you were forty. And now you're still saying you're forty!"

"I'm not," he answered, "the kind of man who changes his word, or takes it back. Isn't that the way a proper man should behave? Even if you ask me twenty years from now, I'll still say exactly the same thing!"

᠁

A friend came to him.

"You promised," the friend said, "to lend me some money. I've come to take you up on it."

"I don't lend my money to anyone," Juha told him. "But, my friend, I'll give you my promises to your heart's content."

᠁

His donkey wandered off, and he swore that, if he found it, he'd sell it for one dinar. When he did find the donkey, he tied a cat to its neck and took the two to the marketplace.

"Who wants," he shouted, "to buy a donkey and a cat for ten dinars? They're a job lot!"

᠁

Juha stopped at the gate to a mill and saw that the donkey turning the wheel had a bell hanging from its neck. He asked the miller why he'd put it there.

"If I should fall asleep," the miller told him, "and the bell stops ringing, then I'll know the donkey's stopped."

"And suppose," Juha asked, "the donkey stops, but moves its head from side to side and makes the bell ring?"

"Get out of here," the miller said, "before you start giving my donkey ideas!"

◆◆◆

A madman once kidnapped a little boy and climbed up with him to the top of a high minaret. People ran after him and were going to climb the minaret too, to save the boy; but he threatened he'd fling the boy down if they followed him. They, perplexed, gathered around the minaret, unsure of what to do.

Juha, learning of the matter, came along and took hold of a large saw.

"If you won't let the boy come down," he shouted to the madman, "I'll saw off the minaret!"

The madman took the bait. Fearful the minaret would fall if Juha did as he'd said, he let the boy come safely down.

◆◆◆

Juha bought three pounds of meat and asked his wife to cook it. This she did, but she ate the meat with some of her relatives. Then, when Juha came and asked for the cooked meat, she told him the cat had eaten it while she was busy preparing other things. Juha took hold of the cat and weighed it; it was, he found, exactly three pounds.

"You cunning woman!" he said to his wife. "If this is the cat, then where's the meat? And if this is the meat, then where's the cat?"

He married a woman who, after just three months, gave birth to a baby. The womenfolk mulled over a name for the newborn child, and Juha suggested "Race Winner."

"Why, Juha?" they asked.

"Well," he answered, "he covers the space of nine months in only three."

⟨⟩

Juha got married to a woman with a face so ugly that, whenever he looked at her, he got depressed and thought he was looking at a man. And then he'd bury his own face in his hands.

One day the wife was looking out of a window and saw a beautiful girl walking down the street. She called Juha over to see the girl, and he heaved a sigh, lamenting his ill fortune. Then he said: "Hey! I've had a wonderful idea!"

"What's that?" his wife asked.

"Why don't the two of us marry her?" Juha suggested.

⟨⟩

Juha had two wives and presented each one separately with a necklace, asking her to keep the gift secret from the other. One day the two of them cornered him and kept asking him which of the two he loved best.

"The one," he said, "that I gave a necklace to as a present."

And so they were both happy and contented, each believing she was the favored one.

❦

A man came to Juha in great perplexity.

"My wife and her sister have quarreled," he said. "They've almost throttled one another. Please, come with me and find some way of patching things up."

"What have they been quarreling about?" Juha inquired. "Their age?"

"No," said the man. "They haven't even mentioned it."

"Go off home then," Juha told him, "and don't worry any more. They've probably made things up by now."

❦

The prince of a certain city was a womanizer, and Juha admonished him, telling him he ought to restrain himself. The prince tried fruitlessly to heed Juha's advice, and ended up tense and withdrawn. One of his bondmaids noticed the change in him and asked what the reason was, and he told her of Juha's admonishment regarding his love of women.

"Give me to him as a gift," she said, "and just see what I'll do to him!"

So, the prince married his bondmaid off to Juha. When Juha was in his private quarters with her, she kept, coquettishly, rejecting his advances, until at last his patience was quite exhausted.

"I won't let you have me," she said, when she saw this, "until you let me put a saddle on your back, and a bit between your teeth, and then mount you."

He agreed to this; whereupon the prince, who'd been secretly waiting, came around and found him in this state.

"What's going on, Juha?" he asked.

"My prince," Juha answered, "this is the fate I was fearing for you—that she'd make a donkey out of you, the way she's just done with me."

⁂

Juha had no love for the governor of his city, and no love, either, for the members of the governor's flattering entourage. And so, he made contact with their enemies. Word of this reached the governor, who thought he'd take this chance to vent his spleen against Juha.

The governor sent for Juha, who denied the accusation. But then a man of the entourage, who happened to be present and was a bitter enemy of Juha's, suggested that Juha's donkey should be let loose at the end of the street. If it took the path toward the enemies' headquarters, then the accusation would be proved true. The animal would be the best possible witness, for donkeys knew the way to places best of all.

The suggestion appealed to the governor, and he put it into effect at once. And the donkey betrayed Juha, going all the way to the headquarters of the governor's enemies. The accusation was upheld accordingly, and Juha knew the penalty would be beheading.

"Suppose, our lord," he said hastily, "that you were to kill me. Do you know what people would say about you?"

"And what would they say?" the governor asked carelessly.

"They'd say," Juha answered, "that you killed an innocent man on the evidence of a donkey—and that only a jackass would rely on evidence like that!"

⁂

One day Juha took the bridle off his donkey's head, and the donkey started bolting this way and that, with Juha powerless to rein it in. So, he surrendered to his donkey's random running, worried only about preserving life and limb. One of his friends saw him in this situation.

"Where are you off to, Juha?" the man shouted.

"Wherever the donkey wants to go, sir," he answered. "Haven't we, after all, decided to let donkeys do our thinking for us?"

⁂

One day Juha was paying homage to a prince.

"How many children do you have?" the prince asked.

"Eight," Juha replied.

The prince accordingly ordered he should receive a grant of eight thousand dirhams. When Juha reached the door, he stopped and turned back.

"Sire," he said, "I forgot to mention one member of my family."

"And who's that?" inquired the prince.

"I myself, sire," said Juha.

And so the prince gave him another thousand dirhams.

A farmer presented a small rabbit to Juha, who was generous to him in return. The farmer thanked him and went off. Next day, two villagers came and awaited Juha's hospitality. He asked them who they were, and they told him they were the neighbors of the man who'd given the rabbit. So, Juha treated them generously, and they left full of gratitude. On the third day, a group of villagers came to him, and he asked them what they wanted. They were, they said, the neighbors of the neighbors of the man who'd given the rabbit. Juha went into the house, came back with a pot of hot water and presented it to them.

"Oh neighbors of the neighbors of the man who gave the rabbit," he said, "this is the sauce of the sauce of the rabbit. You can have it to keep."

A punctilious person asked Juha what was the best position to take in a funeral procession. Was it ahead of the coffin or behind it?

"As long as you're not in the coffin," Juha said, "you can walk wherever you like."

He was eating his meal heartily, and someone interrupted him.

"Why are you eating like that," the man asked, "with five fingers?"

"Because," came Juha's prompt reply, "I don't have six!"

Juha met a friend of his father's.

"Son!" the fellow exclaimed. "Your father had a great beard. Why don't you have any hair on your chin?"

"I take after my mother," Juha replied.

Juha was asked if a man over a hundred years old, who married a young girl, could father a child.

"Yes," he answered. "If he has a neighbor who's twenty or thirty."

Someone hired Juha, then working as a porter, to carry a container with three big bottles in it. On the way, he said, he'd teach Juha three pieces of wisdom that would stand him in good stead.

Juha started carrying the container, and, when they'd gone a third of the way, asked the man to teach him the first piece of wisdom.

"If anyone tells you," the man answered, "that it's better to be hungry than to be full, don't believe him."

Juha agreed this was true. Then, when they'd gone two-thirds of the way, he asked the man to teach him the second piece of wisdom.

"If anyone tells you," the man said, "that walking's better than riding, don't believe him."

Again Juha agreed this was true. When they reached the door of the man's house, Juha asked for the third piece of wisdom.

"If anyone tells you," the man said, "you'll be paid a fee for carrying these bottles, don't believe him."

Juha flung the container down on the ground.

"If anyone tells you," he said, "that there's a single bottle in there that isn't broken, don't believe him!"

❧

Juha attended a banquet given by a wealthy person, and a grilled kid was set in front of him. He started eating with gusto.

"From the way you're tearing into that," remarked the host, who had a malicious streak, "I wonder if the poor creature's mother ever gored you."

"From the sympathy you're showing for it," Juha retorted, "people might think its mother had nursed you at her breast."

❧

Three monks were going around the country, looking for scholars to debate with, and wherever they went, they had the upper hand. Finally they reached Juha's town.

They asked if the place had a scholar in it, and the townsfolk summoned Juha, who arrived riding on his donkey.

"Where's the center of the earth?" the first monk asked him.

"Just where my donkey's put its right foreleg," Juha answered. "If you don't believe me, then you'll have to measure the earth."

The monk was confounded. But then the second monk asked Juha: "How many stars are there?"

"As many," came Juha's answer, "as there are hairs on my donkey. If you don't believe me, count the stars and then count the number of hairs on my donkey."

"How can you count the number of hairs on a donkey?" asked the monk.

"And how," Juha retorted, "can you count the number of stars in the sky?"

Then the third monk asked Juha: "How many hairs are there in my beard?"

"There are as many hairs in your beard," Juha answered promptly, "as there are hairs in my donkey's tail. If you don't believe me, then pluck a hair from your beard and a hair from my donkey's tail. If they come to the same number, then I'm right. If not, it's you that's right."

The monks laughed at these quick, neat answers and admired Juha's presence of mind.

༺༻

When Tamerlane [the infamous tyrant] was in the city of Aaq Shahr, a scholar came to him and suggested he should pose some questions, using signs only, to test the scholars of the city. Tamerlane convened the city's notables, then asked them to nominate someone to face the scholar.

They agreed to consult Juha; and so, they called for him and advised him of the matter.

"Leave it to me," he said. "I'll debate with this scholar in person. If I answer him correctly, and win, then all's well. If I fail, then say I'm just an idiot you never regarded as a scholar anyway. And then bring someone else."

On a particular day, they all assembled in

Tamerlane's presence, and Juha came and sat to his right. The scholar stood up, drew a circle, then gazed full at Juha, waiting for his answer. Juha rose, placed his cane in the exact center of the circle, then drew with it to make two halves. He looked at the scholar; then he divided the circle into quarters, and signaled one quarter as going in one direction and the remaining three quarters as going in another direction. The scholar looked at him with admiration.

The scholar then opened his hands and pointed upward with them. Juha did just the opposite, pointing his fingers toward the earth. Then the scholar placed his fingers on the ground, and started using them to imitate the way animals walk; and he pointed to his belly, as though taking something out from it. Juha took an egg from his pocket and started moving his hands as though he was flying.

The scholar, full of admiration for Juha, approached him, kissed his hands and congratulated Tamerlane and the city's notables on possessing such a distinguished, peerless scholar. When most of those present had gone off, some people told the scholar they hadn't understood the signs exchanged between him and Juha. Would he, they asked, please explain them?

"By the circle," the scholar said, "I meant that the earth's round. Juha endorsed this, drawing a line to show it has a northern half and a southern half. Then he divided it into four quarters, and showed that one quarter represents dry land, while three quarters represent water. I pointed upward with my hands, from the ground, to show that, from the land, trees and plants sprout up. With his hands he pointed downward, to show how the falling of the rains and the heat of the sun help create life on earth. I gave him an indication that creatures multiply through reproduction; and he produced the egg from his pocket as a sign that this is indeed so, and to indicate that, from eggs, birds are created."

The hearers found these explanations good, and called down God's blessings on the scholar. Then they went to Juha and asked him about the signs he'd exchanged with the scholar.

"The man's hungry," Juha said. "You've just wasted my time with him. He showed he had a round loaf of bread, so I made a sign for him to divide it in half between the two of us. When he didn't understand that, I signaled for him to divide it into quarters, with one to go to him and three to me. He nodded to show he agreed, then signed to a pot of rice cooking over a fire; and I signed to him that he needed to put pistachio nuts and raisins in it. Then he walked on all fours to show just how hungry he was, and how he longed for some tasty food. So, I signaled to him that I was even hungrier than he was, and that, when I woke up this morning to have breakfast, all I found was that one egg my wife gave me. I hadn't had time to eat it, because you'd sent asking for me; and so I'd put it in my pocket for when I wanted it."

The people laughed, marveling at the two different interpretations. Yet the signs had been the same.

❧

One day Juha was passing close to a valley when a shepherd came up to him.

"Are you a scholar, sir?" the shepherd asked. Juha told him he was.

"Look at that valley," the shepherd went on,

"and all the people lying there dead. I've killed them all for claiming to be scholars, then failing to answer one simple question."

"And what is the question?" Juha asked.

"It's this," the shepherd said. "When the moon's a crescent, we see that it's small. Then it gets bigger, until in the end it's full. Then it starts getting smaller, until finally it disappears and a new moon starts rising. What do they do with the old moon?"

Juha cleared his throat.

"What ignorant people those were!" he said. "Wasn't there a single one who knew what happens—that the old moons are put in store until winter, then they're pounded into thin strips to make lightning from them?"

At that the shepherd fell over Juha's hand, kissing it.

"Well done, by God!" he cried. "That's just the idea I had!"

Then he gave Juha a sheep as a gift.

꿈

One day Juha was asked: "What do you have to say about divine power?"

"From my earliest recollections," he replied, "I've known that what God decrees will come to pass. But for the influence of divine power, I would have done some of the things I wanted to!"

꿈

"Where's the place of right?" he was asked.

"Is there a place without any right," he asked, "to help you find the other place?"

One day they asked him: "Do you know of anyone in the town who can keep a secret?"

"I've learned peoples' breasts aren't warehouses," he said. "So I haven't told my secrets to anyone in the first place."

He was asked to count the madmen in the town.

"There's no end to the madmen," he answered. "I'll count the sane people if you like. There aren't too many of them."

Asked about medicine, he replied: "The great secret is to keep your feet warm, expose your head to the air and the sun, be careful what you eat and don't overeat, and don't dwell on your worries and griefs."

"You know," one of his neighbors said, "how silly and headstrong my daughter is. Would you recite some Quranic verses over her and make her an amulet?"

"An old man reciting Quranic verses won't do any good," he answered. "Just look for a man of twenty-five or thirty to be a husband and wise man at the same time. Once she has children, she'll be wise and obedient."

✿✿✿

Once, when attending the court of his city's governor, Juha was asked: "Is it true contentment's a treasure that never grows less?"

"Yes, it is," he answered. "But it's not a treasure that feeds hungry people or clothes people dressed in rags. You only find it in people who don't work."

✿✿✿

Juha had two wives. One evening, when he was sitting with them and enjoying their company, they decided to trap him by asking which one of them he loved the best.

"I love you both the same," he told them.

"Oh, no," they said, "you can't just slither out of it like that. You're in trouble this time! Now, there's a pool over there. Just choose which of us you'd rather drown in it. Which one of us are you going to toss in the water?"

Juha hesitated, pondering his dilemma. Finally he turned to his first wife.

"I've just remembered, my dear," he said. "You learned to swim some years back, didn't you?"

✿✿✿

"Which way does a swimmer face," someone asked Juha, "once he's in the water?"

"He faces the direction where he left his clothes," Juha answered.

Juha came across an acquaintance in the street.

"Hey," the man said, "I've just seen a messenger carrying a table loaded with piles of food."

"So, what does that have to do with me?" Juha asked.

"They took it to your house," the friend replied.

"So," Juha said, "what does that have to do with you?"

A man hit Juha from behind in the middle of the street, looking to make fun of him. Juha grabbed the man by the collar and dragged him in front of the judge. The man claimed he'd mistaken Juha for a friend of his, someone he often joked with in this heavy-handed way. Juha, though, refused to accept his apology.

The judge knew the offender personally, and wanted to spare him any punishment. The best thing to do, he declared, was for Juha to hit the man in the same way, or else agree to take ten dirhams from him by way of compensation. Juha couldn't resist the lure of the money, and the judge asked the man if he had it with him.

The offender saw what the judge was driving at. He didn't, he said, have the money with him, but he'd go home and bring it back right away. The judge gave him permission to leave, and he didn't return. After a long wait, Juha got wise to the judge's ruse. He came up close to the judge, as if to whisper in his ear, then gave him a mighty slap. As he left, he said: "If by any chance the man comes back with the money, then I hereby waive it in your favor."

※

Juha was taking a grilled goose to the prince, and on the way he was so overcome by hunger, and the aroma of the grilled meat, that he ate one of the legs.

He handed the goose to the prince, who asked where the missing leg had gone.

"It hasn't gone anywhere," Juha told him. "The geese in this town are all one-legged."

With that he led the prince to one of the castle windows and showed him a line of geese all standing on one leg, the way geese do when resting. The prince thereupon turned to a soldier among his bodyguard and ordered him to chase the geese off with his staff. The moment the soldier did this, the geese went scurrying in all directions, on their two legs.

"You see?" said the prince. "These are local geese too, and they're born with two legs—not just one!"

"One moment, my dear prince," Juha replied. "If a soldier with a staff like that were to threaten a man, and not a goose, the man would take off on four legs, not just two."

※

Juha was selling his olive crop, and a woman was haggling with him. She thought the price he was asking was too high.

"Look," she said, "why don't you sell them to me at the higher price I offered, to be paid later on. You know my husband, so-and-so."

Juha handed her a single olive, so she could taste its quality and see his price was a fair one. She, though, wouldn't do this. She was fasting, she said, because she'd been sick a year earlier and hadn't fasted during Ramadan.

"That settles it, then," Juha said. "If you can put God off for a whole year, you'd be quite capable of putting me off until Judgment Day!"

❧

One day Juha was taking a stroll outside the town, in front of a cemetery. He saw a troop of horsemen coming toward him and took fright. Then, seeing an open grave right in front of him, he had the bright idea of hiding inside, and so he took off his outer garments and hopped in. When the horsemen came up and saw him there in the grave, half naked, they could hardly believe their eyes.

"You there!" they said. "What do you think you're doing down in that grave?"

He couldn't think what to say. At last he managed to gather his wits.

"I'm a member of the grave community," he said. "But I got bored, being down here so long. So I asked God's permission to wander out for a while, and He agreed."

The horsemen just laughed and left him to his own devices.

❧

Someone complained of a bad cold, and another person heard him.

"I just don't understand these people," the second person said, in Juha's hearing. "When winter comes, they complain about the cold. When summer comes, they complain about the heat. They're never happy."

"That's quite true," Juha put in. "But did you ever hear anyone complain about the spring?"

❧

Juha dropped in on a family while they were eating.

"Who are you?" they asked.

"I'm the rude fellow," he answered, "who saves you the bother of sending a messenger to invite him."

❧

A beggar rapped at Juha's door.

"Who's there?" Juha called.

"Come on down," said the beggar. So Juha went down.

"Give me some alms," the beggar said, "for the sake of God."

"Come in," Juha said, "and follow me."

The beggar followed him right up onto the roof, where Juha said: "God will provide."

"And why," the beggar retorted, "didn't you say that when I was down at your front door?"

"And why," Juha rejoined, "didn't you ask for alms when I was up here?"

❧

He claimed to be a saint.

"All right," the people said. "What miracle can you perform?"

"I know what's in your hearts," he told them.

"So," they answered, "what is it? Tell us."

"In his heart," he replied, "each one of you's thinking I'm a liar."

"You're dead right," they all agreed.

⁂

Juha's friends made an agreement with him. If he spent a whole winter night out in the wilderness, and didn't make a fire to warm himself, then they'd treat him to a banquet. If he couldn't keep his end of the bargain, then he was to throw a banquet for them. Juha agreed, and stayed up all night in the wilderness, shifting stones from one place to another to keep himself warm.

Morning arrived, and his friends came up to him.

"How did you manage to stand the cold?" they asked him.

"I saw a ray of light a mile off," he told them, joking as usual, "and I used that to keep warm."

They cried out with one voice.

"You cheated! You broke the terms, Juha. Now you have to treat us to a banquet."

He tried his utmost to convince them, but they wouldn't budge. Finally they all agreed to hold the dinner in three days.

The time duly came around, and the people all showed up, expecting food. Noon came, the afternoon passed, and still no food appeared. Why, they asked him, was he so late with the lunch?

"Come with me," he answered. "You'll see, it isn't properly cooked yet."

They went with him, to the courtyard of his house, and there they saw he'd hung a pot at the top of a palm tree, and put a small stove right down on the ground.

"What do you think you're doing," they shrieked, "trying to bring that pot to the boil with a small stove like this, such a long way away from it?"

"You people have pretty short memories," Juha retorted. "Only three days ago you pretended to believe I'd warmed myself with a ray of light a mile away. So, what makes you think the pot can't come to the boil, when it's only a few yards from the stove?"

※

Juha, then a beggar, stopped at the door of a wealthy Turk with many servants and begged for alms. The Turk was sitting on the terrace of his mansion.

"Coral," the Turk told one of his servants, "tell Turquoise to tell Ruby to tell this beggar: 'May God provide for you from someone else, not from here.'"

Juha, furious, raised his hands high.

"Oh, God!" he prayed. "Tell the angel Israfil to tell the angel Mikal to tell 'Izra'il: 'Reap the soul of this miserly Turk!'"

[NOTE: Israfil is the angel of the Last Judgment, Mikal (Michael) the providing angel and 'Izra'il the angel of death.]

※

An irritating man asked Juha to lend him his donkey to carry out some tasks. Juha's donkey was very dear to him, and he knew, if the donkey struggled under its load or stumbled along the way, that this fat man would probably heap curses and damnation on donkey and owner alike.

So, Juha told him, with apologies, that another friend had borrowed the donkey earlier, to help with his own tasks. The man had no option but to accept the excuse. Then, just as he was leaving, the donkey started braying in the courtyard of the house.

The man was furious.

"Are you telling me, Juha," he inquired sarcastically, "that the donkey isn't here, and yet there it is, braying inside?"

Juha decided to cap the man's cheek with something even cheekier.

"Take it easy, friend," he said. "I've had my say and the donkey's had his. Aren't you ashamed of yourself, accepting the donkey's say-so and calling an old gray-bearded man a liar?"

෴

No sooner had the previous man left than another came to ask for the use of Juha's donkey. Juha was irritated, but he was afraid of using the same excuse, only for the donkey to show him up a second time. So, he asked the man to wait for a moment, then went inside.

"I'm sorry, friend," he said, when he returned. "I've consulted the donkey on the matter, and he refuses to go with you. 'I serve men,' he told me, 'and carry their loads. And all I get from them is curses and beating.'"

"When did donkeys start talking, Juha?" asked the astonished man. "And since when have they had opinions?"

"You see it and hear it all the time," Juha answered promptly. "Aren't there any number of [two-legged] donkeys who talk? Aren't they consulted, then give their opinions?"

. 2 .

Social Satire

One day Juha announced that, the following Friday in the late afternoon, he'd fly off from the top of the minaret of the Great Mosque in Kufa. When the time came, people flocked there expectantly, from far and wide. The square was crammed with a vast crowd.

Juha, on his pinnacle, looked scornfully down at them. Then he started waving his arms in the air, flapping them around as if he were getting ready to fly. Time passed, but still he didn't fly off, and they called out to him to keep his word. He gazed at them sarcastically.

"I thought no one," he said, "could be as naïve and stupid as I am. Now I see you're just as stupid. In fact some of you look to be even stupider—people who believe things even Juha couldn't swallow. You're taken in by things that don't even fool me any more—you think the impossible can happen. Tell me, all you clever men, how do you suppose someone like me—or you—could fly without any wings?"

❧

Some people told Juha his wife had lost her brains. He thought for a few moments.

"She doesn't have any brains," he said finally. "Let me think now, what might she have lost?"

Juha and his wife were sitting at dinner, which included a very hot soup. His wife took some soup, and it scalded her mouth, making her eyes water. When Juha asked her why, she said she'd remembered her late mother and that had started her weeping. Then Juha took a little soup and scalded his own mouth, and his eyes started watering too. His wife asked him why he had tears in his eyes.

"I'm mourning your late mother," he said. "She was born malicious like you, and then you left her to make me miserable!"

When Juha's wife passed away, he married a widow who regularly brought up the merits of her late husband. And, to spite her, he in his turn would recount the numerous merits of his late wife.

Finally he grew tired of all this. One night, when they were sleeping, he kicked her out of bed and she fell onto the floor. Furious, she went to complain to her father.

"I hope you won't judge me too harshly," Juha told him. "There are four of us sleeping in the same bed: my late wife and myself, and your daughter and her late husband. There isn't room in the bed for four, so your daughter rolled out on the floor. Surely you can't blame me for that?"

A matchmaker arranged for Juha to marry a woman who was very ugly, and he saw her for the first time on their wedding night. When morning came, she turned shyly to him.

"Tell me, please," she said coquettishly. "Which of your male relations should I show myself to, and which ones should I hide myself from?"

"Show yourself to everybody," he answered. "Just stay hidden from me!"

Juha was critically ill.

"Go and put on your smartest clothes and most attractive make-up," he told his wife. "Then come back here to me."

"How can I leave your side," she asked, "when you're here on your death bed? Do you think I'm ungrateful or weak-willed?"

"No, my dear," Juha said. "You missed my meaning. I can see the angel of death hovering over me. Perhaps if he saw you in your splendid clothes, and looking so attractive, he might leave me and take you instead!"

Juha recounted: "A friend asked me once: 'Why not marry, Juha?' 'I'd divorce my own self,' I told him, 'if only I could.'"

Juha wanted to build a house. So, he told the carpenter to use the ceiling wood for the floor and the floor wood for the ceiling. The carpenter asked him why this was.

"They say," Juha answered, "that when you get married everything's turned upside down, and I'm getting married soon myself. This way, everything will turn back to normal."

When Juha was a judge, an old woman was brought before him to testify in a case. Juha instructed her to take the oath.

"I swear by Almighty God," the woman said, "to tell the truth."

He then asked her how old she was.

"If you were going to ask me that," the old woman retorted, "why tell me to swear by Almighty God?"

One day Juha was riding his donkey and his son was following him on foot. A group of people passed by.

"Look at that man," they commented, "riding and letting his son walk. Doesn't he have any pity?"

So, Juha dismounted and let his son ride the donkey, while he walked along behind. Another group of people passed by.

"Look at that lad," they commented, "riding the donkey while his father walks. Doesn't he have any manners?" So, Juha mounted the donkey together with his son, and they went on their way. They passed by a third group of people.

"Look at that heartless man," they commented, "riding the donkey along with his son. Doesn't he have any pity for the beast?"

So, Juha and his son both dismounted and walked, driving the donkey on ahead of them. They passed yet another group of people.

"Look at those two imbeciles," they said, "tiring themselves out walking, and there's the donkey in front of them without any load."

So, Juha and his son carried the donkey between them, and walked along like this. They passed still another group of people.

"Look at these two madmen," they said, "carrying the donkey instead of letting the donkey carry them."

At that the two of them let the donkey fall.

"Let me tell you something, son," Juha said. "You can never please everyone!"

❧

Juha and his son were standing alongside as a funeral procession passed. The widow was lamenting, and addressing her dead husband.

"They're taking you," she said, "to a place where there's no bed, or cover, or carpet, or food, or water."

"By Almighty God, father," Juha's son said, "it's our house they're going to!"

❧

Juha sent his son to buy him some grapes, but the son was away so long that Juha lost patience. When the boy finally came back with the grapes, Juha asked him about the figs.

"But," the son said, "you didn't ask me to get any figs."

"When I send you to do one thing for me," Juha instructed him, "you ought to do two!"

Some time after this, Juha fell ill and told his son to fetch a doctor. So, the son brought a doctor and another man along with him.

"Who's this second fellow?" Juha asked.

"Didn't you tell me," the son answered, "that, whenever you ask me to do one thing, I ought to do two? So, I brought you the doctor and, if he cures you, that's fine. If he doesn't, I brought the grave digger too."

&⊕&

Juha's mother-in-law went to the river bank to do her washing. Her foot slipped, and she fell in the river and drowned. People hurried to look for her body, but they couldn't find it, and they went to tell Juha, who came and started looking for the body upstream from where she'd fallen in.

"But," they told him, "her body would have gone downstream, with the current, not upstream."

"Let me be," he said. "I know what she was like. You wouldn't believe how contrary she was."

&⊕&

Juha sold his wife's anklet, then went off toward the marketplace to buy a donkey with the money. An ill-omened man met him and asked him where he was going.

"To buy a donkey," Juha said.

"Say 'God willing,' Juha," the man told him. Juha, as the man knew well enough, was pious and believed in God's will. Still, his intrusion upset Juha.

"Why tell me to do that," he asked, "when the money's in my pocket and the donkeys are in the market?"

With that Juha went on to the market, where a thief picked his pocket. On his way back, without money or donkey, he passed by the same ill-omened man.

"Where are you coming from, Juha?" the man asked.

"From the marketplace, God willing," Juha answered furiously. "My money was stolen, God willing. And may a curse fall on your mother and father, God willing!"

(Finally, though—true to the popular saying that "some people's disasters are other people's benefits"— Juha came to own a donkey when the imam of the village mosque passed away without any heirs, and Juha inherited both the imam's job and donkey.)

⁂

Juha's wife passed away, but he didn't shed any tears over her. Then his donkey died, and he wouldn't stop weeping. People were amazed at the state he was in.

"What on earth is this all about, Juha?" people asked. "Your wife passed away, and you never wept for her. Then your donkey dies, and you're forever in tears."

"You people!" Juha answered. "How can you blame me? When my wife passed away, this man said his sister would make me the best of wives, and that man said his daughter would be the best solace for my wife's loss—he'd marry her off to me without any payment. But when my donkey died, not a soul offered me any consolation at all."

❧

"How long," someone asked him, "will people go on being born and dying?"

"Until hell's full," Juha replied.

❧

The governor ordered Juha to make a census of all the madmen in the country.

"At your service," Juha said. "But I've already made a census of the scholars, and they claim everyone else in the country's crazy. That's just too many for me to count."

❧

An illiterate fellow received a letter written in Persian. Some time later he ran into Juha.

"Could you read this letter for me," he asked, "and tell me what it says?"

Juha took the letter, and, finding it was in Persian, gave it back to the man.

"Find someone else to read it for you," he said.

The illiterate man, though, insisted that it had to be Juha who read the letter.

"My mind's confused," Juha said. "I've had a quarrel with my wife. This is in Persian, but even if it had been in Arabic, I couldn't have read it—not in the state I am now."

The man became angry.

"If you don't even know how to read," he retorted, "why do you put that big turban on your head, and wear that scholar's cloak, and dress up like a shaikh?"

Annoyed at this, Juha flung the turban and the cloak at the man.

"If being able to read," he said, "is a matter of a turban and a scholar's cloak, then put these on, and let's hear you read a couple of lines from that letter!"

✦✦

Juha was always complaining about the people in his town, telling everyone he met—whether from the town itself or outside—how stupid and two-faced his fellow townspeople were.

This provoked regular condemnation and resentment from the townsfolk themselves. And then he'd try to convince his critics through some physical incident he'd call them to witness. Once he tore the door off his house and hoisted it up on his back. Then he told one of his loudest critics: "Just come with me, and count."

At a bend in the road, one of his fellow townsmen called out, laughing: "What's that you're carrying on your back, Juha?"

"There's one for a start," Juha told his companion. "Just look! A great long, wide door, and he doesn't even know what it is!"

≪≛≫

He complained to his landlord that he could hear noises up on the roof.

"Don't worry," said the landlord. "It's just someone praising God."

"That's what I'm afraid of," Juha replied. "Worship starts off quietly enough. But if the piety really gets hold of him, then maybe he'll prostrate himself in humility to God, and bring the roof down on top of us."

≪≛≫

One day Shaikh Nasruddin [Juha] was standing in the pulpit of a mosque in Aaq Shahr.

"You believers!" he said. "Do you know what I'm going to say to you?"

"No," the hearers answered. "We've no idea."

"Well," Juha said, "if you don't know, I may as well keep quiet."

With that he went off, but came back another day. He flung the same question at the hearers, and this time they said they did know.

"Well," Juha said, "if you know what I'm going to say, I may as well keep quiet."

The hearers were nonplussed at this. Next time, they decided, they'd give two conflicting answers. One group would answer "no" and the other group "yes."

Back came Juha for the third time and asked the crowd the same question. And, as they'd agreed, their answers were split.

"That's fine then," said Juha. "The ones who know had better tell the ones who don't."

Juha was out on the road and ravenously hungry. So, he sat down in the shade of a tree and started eating some of the food he had with him. An acquaintance of his—a stupid, pretentious man—passed by, and, instead of greeting him, just stood there staring.

"What are you doing, Juha?" he asked.

"The same as anyone else," Juha answered.

"Not at all," the man said. "What you're doing isn't respectable."

"How do you mean?" Juha asked.

"My dear fellow," the man said, "it's just not done to eat by the side of the road, the way you're doing. It lowers you in people's eyes."

Juha laughed in inward derision.

"What people are you talking about?" he asked.

"The ones passing by here," the man said.

"Those aren't people," Juha answered. "They're cattle."

The man resented this, and Juha thought it better not to get into a quarrel with him. He didn't want other people to hear what they'd been saying and hold it against him. After a while, his wit found him a clinching argument.

"Just a moment, brother," he said, getting up. "Don't be impatient. Just wait." He went up onto higher ground, then called out at the top of his voice:

"You people! I'm going to preach to you. Listen carefully!"

People came flocking from all directions, and he started his sermon:

"Oh, sons of Adam!" he warned. "You're like beasts of the field, only you've gone still further astray. You're brands for the flames of hell on Judgment Day!"

Every last one of them had a teardrop on his cheek, or bowed his head in sorrow over his state. Juha went on, pouring out tales of bygone peoples, until he'd run out of things to tell them.

"You people!" he concluded. "It's been passed down to us that whoever puts out his tongue and touches the tip of his nose with it, God will forgive him his sins, both past and to come."

Not one of them kept his tongue inside his mouth. Juha left them like that and turned to his companion.

"Look at that, you imbecile!" he said. "Are those people or cattle?"

❦

Juha was invited to a banquet. He went there wearing tattered clothes, and no one paid him any consideration. So, he went home, put on some fine clothes, mounted a mule and went back to the banquet. He was received with respect: people made much of him and had him sit down in the front part of the hall.

When the food was brought in, he draped his sleeve over it, and said, "Eat, oh sleeve!" The people there were astonished.

"All the consideration you paid me," Juha said, "was for my sleeve, not for me as a person. So, the sleeve has a better right to the food than I do."

One day Juha went to the public bath. The clothes he was wearing didn't arouse any respect, and he was treated without consideration. They gave him an old towel, and didn't provide the proper service. When he'd finished, he gave them a very large fee. They were astonished and delighted.

The following week he went there, and met with a hearty welcome and great respect: they supplied him with clean towels and lavished the utmost care on him. When he'd finished, he gave them, to their fury, a most meager sum.

"That's no fair reward," they cried, "for everything we did for you!"

"Don't get annoyed," he said. "Just apply today's fee to last time, and last time's fee to today."

He cooked a meal and sat down with his wife to eat.

"How tasty this meal would be," he said, "if it wasn't for the crowd."

"What crowd?" his wife asked. "There are only the two of us here."

"It used to be just me and the pot," Juha replied.

Juha had a gluttonous guest. He put four loaves in front of the man, then went to fetch the main dish, which was of lentils. By the time he returned, the man had finished off all four loaves. Juha put the lentils down in front of the man and went off to get more bread. When he got back, he found the man had eaten the lentils. This went on until Juha had no more bread or lentils left in the house.

"Brother," Juha asked the man, "where are you going off to after this?"

"To Baghdad," the man answered. "There's an expert doctor there, and I want him to treat my stomach. I don't seem to be eating as much as usual."

"Well," Juha told him, "I pray to God, if you find him and have him give your stomach the room it had before, that you'll plan your journey back by another route. If not, let me know in advance, so I can leave before you get here."

❧

One day there was a strong wind raging. People started praying to God and reciting parts of the Quran.

"All right, all right," Juha told them. "Don't be in too much of a hurry to repent. It's only a storm. It'll pass."

❧

Juha was traveling. When he decided he needed a rest, he sat down under a tree, and suddenly saw, on the other side of the trunk, an old man weeping bitterly with a dog lying on the ground next to him. Feeling sorry for the man, he went up, as he usually did, to see if he could help in any way.

The man at once answered through his tears, in a shaky voice.

"My dog," he said. "My dog! He's been my faithful

companion, when friends have betrayed me. I can't bear to see him in this dreadful state."

"What's wrong with your dog, sir?" Juha asked.

"The poor creature's at death's door," said the man, "because it hasn't had anything to eat."

Now, Juha had no food to give the dog, so he tried to console and comfort the man. After a while, though, he noticed a bulging knapsack next to the man.

"What's that in the knapsack, brother?" he asked.

"Some loaves of bread," the man answered, "that I'm carrying as provisions."

"What kind of way is that to behave?" Juha asked. "All that bread, and you won't give any to save the life of your precious, faithful dog?"

The man stared at him.

"Really, sir!" he said. "Yes, it is precious and it is faithful, but our bond doesn't stretch as far as the mouth of this knapsack!"

❧

He went out once, seeking his livelihood, and came to a town where the whole population had, it seemed, embraced righteousness in every possible way. So, Juha preached to them. He'd hardly finished his sermon when they all started sobbing tearfully, and tugging at their beards as a mark of penitence. As he stepped down from the pulpit, expecting a respectful reception, he chanced to look around for his Quran, and couldn't find it. He looked with new eyes at all these sobbing, righteous people.

"I see," he said, "how you're all weeping in penitence for your sins. Now, which penitent stole my Quran?"

A particular notable used to show Juha great admiration; whenever they met, he'd lavish flattering phrases and choice words on him. So, Juha decided he'd like to pay the man a visit.

As he arrived at the notable's house, the man was looking out of the window. Then, seeing Juha approaching, he promptly pulled back into the house. Juha knocked on the door.

"Tell the professor," he said, "I've come to visit him—if it's not troubling him too much."

"Oh," he was told, "the professor went out a short time back. He'll be so sorry to hear you honored him with a visit when he wasn't at home."

On hearing this, Juha called out in a loud voice: "Very well. But please give the professor a piece of advice from me. Next time he goes out of the house, he shouldn't leave his head behind in the window. People might think he was at home and say he was ill-mannered!"

. 3 .

Cunning and Resource

Juha met a woman who asked him where he'd just come from. He'd come, he told her, from Gehenna. She immediately asked him if he'd seen her dead son. Yes, Juha said, he had indeed seen him, standing at the gate of Paradise, to which he wouldn't be allowed entry until his debts were repaid—specifically, some money owed to Juha. The woman gave Juha the sum in question, then went off home, where she happily recounted what had happened to her husband.

The man left the house and rode off on his horse, in search of the swindling Juha. When Juha saw him coming, he went hurrying into a mill, and told the miller a man was pursuing the miller himself [for some misdeed]. If the miller wanted to save himself, he should change clothes with Juha, then climb up in a tree and hide among its branches. The miller followed Juha's advice.

When the husband arrived, and went into the mill in search of the man who'd swindled him, Juha pointed out the man who'd climbed the tree. The husband promptly took off his robes and climbed up himself, in pursuit of the thief; whereupon Juha took the robes, mounted the man's horse and fled.

The husband got back home at last. And there he told his wife the man had indeed come down from heaven, and that he himself had left the man his robes and horse to take to their son along with the money!

One day the Sultan, wishing to honor Juha and treat him graciously, told him: "Advise me of your desire, and you shall have it."

"My lord Sultan," Juha replied, "there is but one thing I desire. This is, that you will decree I may take a jackass from every man who lives in fear of his wife."

The Sultan agreed to Juha's request and issued orders to that effect.

A few days later, the Sultan saw Juha walking down the street, driving in front of him a herd of so many jackasses that the dust they raised filled the city. So the Sultan had Juha brought before him and inquired into the matter.

"In accordance with your decree," Juha said, "whenever I saw a man who was afraid of his wife, I took a jackass from him."

The Sultan was struck with wonder and amusement together, to hear that so many men feared their wives.

"I saw," Juha told the Sultan then, "in one of the neighboring cities, a girl as lovely as the full moon, her figure as though it were the slenderest of willow branches, with fresh cheeks, rosy lips, teeth like pearls set together, a neck like a decanter of silver or crystal—"

"Not so loud, Juha," the Sultan broke in, "in case my wife hears you! She's so jealous, and she leads me a terrible life. She's close by this room. I'm afraid she might hear you."

Juha got up, laughing.

"If," he said, "I'm to take one jackass from every man of the populace who's afraid of his wife, then you, my lord, should send me two."

Juha stopped by a merchant's shop and started haggling over the price of some cloth to make a robe. He wouldn't, he said, pay more than thirty dirhams. Then he remembered he already had a new robe.

"I did mean to have a new robe made," he told the merchant, "but I've changed my mind. Give me, instead, a piece of good cloth that's enough to make a cloak."

The merchant gave him the cloth, and Juha took it and started walking off.

"Hey, shaikh," the merchant shouted after him, "you haven't paid me for that cloth you've taken for the cloak!"

"What on earth do you mean?" Juha retorted. "Didn't I leave you the cloth for the robe instead?"

"But," said the merchant, "you didn't give me the money for that either."

Juha's face filled with amazement.

"Great is the Lord!" he exclaimed. "I didn't even take the cloth for the robe, so why should I pay you for it?"

A fellow claimed that nobody could dupe or deceive him. So, Juha went to him.

"You reckon," he said, "there's nobody able to dupe or deceive you?"

"Yes," the man replied simply, with supreme arrogance.

"Well," said Juha, "here I am to challenge you—to show I can dupe you. I'm going to show you up as a fool, to everyone."

"No one can do that," the man replied. "Still, if you think you can, then go ahead and try."

"Would you like to bet on it?" asked Juha.

"Yes," said the man. "I'll make a bet with you."

"We can really only do things out in the open," Juha said. "Let's go out, and I'll show you how deception works."

The man agreed, and went out with Juha to the open fields.

There was a strong wind, and it was threatening to rain. When they'd gone some way out of town, Juha saw, in the distance, a man on a donkey.

"Really," Juha told his companion, "I can't get the better of you unless we have a gathering of people, so they can judge between us. Just wait here while I go and fetch some people. I'll ride on the donkey behind this man, and bring them right back." His companion agreed.

So, Juha went off home and sat there, warm and cozy, while the man stayed out in the stormy wind and bitter cold. The rain started pouring down, and in the end he got tired of waiting and started to shiver from the cold. When night set in, and still Juha hadn't come back, the arrogant man returned to town, muttering curses and damnation, and went straight to Juha's house to tell him just what he thought of him, for leaving him standing out so long in the stormy cold and the rain. But Juha said:

"That, Mr. Clever Fellow, who's seen everything, was the deception. Get off now, and don't be so ready to claim nobody can fool you."

Juha sold his house, all except for a nail in one of the walls — that, he specified, wasn't part of the sale. He made it a condition, too, that he could go and visit his nail freely, at any time whatever, because it was so dear to him. The buyer agreed to this.

Next morning, at breakfast time, Juha went to visit his nail, and the man invited him to breakfast. Then, around noon, at lunch time, along came Juha to feast his eyes on his nail, and the man invited him to lunch. And that evening, when supper time came, there was Juha yet again, to inspect the nail, and the man invited him to supper. Even at times of rest and the time for sleep, Juha would suddenly appear, to find out what was happening with the nail.

So things went on, until finally the buyer could stand it no longer. Yet, by the terms of the contract, he had to let Juha come. When all his ruses failed to rid him of the visits, he surrendered the whole house to Juha and moved out, without getting back a penny of the cash he'd paid.

He borrowed a big cooking pot from one of his neighbors and used it to prepare his food. Then he put a small pot inside it, and gave it back.

"What's this, Juha?" the neighbor asked. "The pot's given birth. Here's its daughter."

Later Juha asked for the big pot again, but hid it once he'd finished with it. In due course the neighbor demanded its return.

"Where's the pot?" he asked.

"It died," Juha said, "while giving birth."

"How can a pot die?" exclaimed the neighbor.

"If a pot can give birth," Juha said, "it can die while it's doing it. My friend, the one who reaps the profit has to bear the loss too!"

***

Every morning Juha would stand in the courtyard of his house, raise his hands to the sky and say: "God, bless me with a thousand dinars. I'll accept nothing less!"

A neighbor heard him and was astonished to see how naïve he was, and he decided to put Juha to the test. So, he put 999 dinars in a bundle, which he then tossed through the window so that it landed in front of Juha. Juha was delighted.

"God," he said, "has given me what I asked for."

Then he counted the money and found it was one dinar short.

"He who has given me so much," he said, "won't deny me a further one dinar later." And with that he put the money in a chest he had.

The neighbor, watching him from a window, was furious. He went to Juha's house and knocked hard on the door. Juha opened.

"What can I do for you?" he asked.

"Bring me that bundle you took!" the neighbor said.

"My Lord," Juha told him, "gave me something. And now you want to take it away from me?"

"I was the one," the neighbor said, "who tossed the bundle in, to see if you really would accept less or not."

They went on arguing. Finally the neighbor said: "I'm not leaving until you agree to come with me to the judge."

Juha agreed. "But," he said, "I'm sick. I can't walk and I'm afraid of the cold. I don't have any warm clothes or any shoes to wear. Give me your donkey to ride on, and some new warm clothes to put on, and some new shoes. Then I'll go with you to the judge."

The neighbor gave him what he'd asked for, and off they went to the judge.

There the neighbor claimed Juha had taken a bundle containing a thousand dinars, all but one, which he'd tossed in front of him to try him out. The judge asked Juha if this was true.

"Is that a plausible claim, your Honor?" Juha slyly answered. "Is it really likely this man, famous for his miserly ways, would toss away 999 dinars? In fact it was money I earned through my own labor. This man's always making false accusations against people—he's well known for it. It's happened plenty of times with the other neighbors. I'm afraid he'll claim too—right here in front of you—that these clothes and new shoes I'm wearing, and this hardy donkey I've ridden coming over here, are all his property too."

"By God, your Honor!" the neighbor cried. "The donkey, and the clothes, and the shoes, really are my property!"

"Didn't I tell you, Honorable Judge," Juha answered, smiling, "that he's notorious for deceiving people and making false accusations against them?"

"I have to say," the judge told the neighbor, "that you're a swindler and a liar. Off with you, or else I'll punish you."

The man left, bitter and regretting what he'd done, while Juha took home his money, his new clothes and his donkey.

*

A neighbor of Juha's had a skinny, misshapen billy goat, which she vainly tried to sell. Juha took pity on her.

"Tomorrow," he told her, "bring it to the marketplace. Then I'll come and haggle with you over how much it's worth. But don't agree to any price under a hundred dinars."

Next day the woman took her goat to the marketplace, and Juha arrived with a measuring tape and started going around the vendors, making calculations. Up he came to the woman, with no sign of recognition, and started measuring the goat from top to bottom, from end to end. People gathered around to watch him—upon which he began haggling with her over the price: up through ten, twenty, thirty dinars, until he finally reached ninety dinars. She, though, refused to settle for anything under a hundred.

Juha said he was sorry, he didn't have that much money, then turned and walked off. At that a merchant came up to her and, having concluded there must be something hugely special about this goat, bought it for a hundred dinars. Then he raced after Juha. Would Juha, he asked, please tell him what special benefit he'd hoped to gain from the goat? Juha sat down and once more took the billy goat's measurements, from every angle.

"If it had been two fingers longer," he told the merchant, "and one finger wider, its skin would have been perfect for a tambourine—or maybe a drum!"

. 4 .

Naïveté and Stupidity

One morning Juha went to the marketplace and bought a donkey. Then he started back home, leading the donkey behind him on a rope. Two thieves followed him, and one of them untied the rope from the donkey's neck and put it around his own, while the other one took off with the donkey. Juha, meanwhile, was quite unaware of what was happening.

After a while Juha happened to look behind him, and saw a man there in place of the donkey.

"Where's the donkey?" he asked, astonished.

"I'm the donkey," the thief answered.

"How's that?" demanded Juha.

"I was ungrateful to my mother," he said, "and so she put a curse on me—she prayed the Almighty would turn me into a donkey. Next morning I woke up to find I really had been turned into one. And she took me off to the marketplace and sold me to the man you just bought me from. It seems, God be praised, that I'm now back in my mother's favor and blessing. I've been turned into a human being again."

"All power is in the Almighty," Juha observed. "How could I have used you, when you were human all the time? Off you go now."

With that, Juha untied the rope from around the thief's neck. "Now," he warned the man, "don't upset your mother again! God will compensate me for my loss."

A week later he went to the marketplace to buy a

donkey, and there was the same one he'd bought the week before. He went up to it.

"You ill-omened donkey!" he whispered in its ear. "You've been ungrateful to your mother again, after I warned you not to be. You deserve everything that's happened to you!"

※

A fellow fainted, and his family thought he was dead. So, they had him washed, shrouded, and carried on a bier for burial. As the funeral procession wound down the road, the man regained consciousness and sat up on the bier.

"I'm alive," he yelled. "I'm not dead at all! Juha, save me!"

"What are you saying?" Juha exclaimed. "Am I supposed to believe you and say all these mourners are wrong?"

※

Juha got married. Three months later his wife told him she was ready to give birth and asked him to go and fetch the midwife.

"What's happening here?" Juha asked. "Women give birth after nine months. Everyone knows that."

She got angry at this.

"Man," she said, "how long have we been married? Three months, isn't it?"

He replied that it was.

"And how long," she went on, "have you been married to me? Three months, isn't it? That makes six in all."

Again, he agreed this was so.

"And how long," she pursued, "has the child been in my womb? Three months, hasn't it? And that makes the full nine months, doesn't it?"

Juha pondered at length.

"Yes," he told her finally, "I was wrong, I'm sorry. I just wasn't counting straight."

*

One day Juha was sitting on the preacher's chair in a mosque, ready to deliver a sermon, and people had flocked there to hear him. Then, suddenly, he found he couldn't find anything to say to the congregation — his mind was empty. The people, meanwhile, were getting annoyed.

"You people!" he told them finally. "You know what a gifted speaker I am. I wanted to address you, but my mind's a blank."

Juha's son was sitting next to his chair.

"Father," he said, "if nothing occurred to you to talk about, didn't it occur to you to get up off the chair?"

*

Juha found an iron shoe, the kind used to shoe donkeys. He was overjoyed at this. If only, he said to himself, he could find three more like it!

"If I do," he thought, "then, God willing, I should have no problem getting hold of a donkey!"

One day Juha got down from his donkey to relieve himself, putting his cloak on top of the saddle. When he came back, he couldn't find the cloak—a passing thief had stolen it. So, Juha started beating the donkey and asking it where the cloak was.

At last he took the saddle off his donkey's back, put it on his own back and started pulling the donkey along.

"When you give me back my cloak," he told the donkey, "you'll get the saddle back!"

One day Juha rode to the marketplace on his donkey. He bought some vegetables, put them in the saddle bag, then, flinging the saddle bag over his shoulders, he mounted the donkey and rode off.

"Why," a friend asked him, "don't you put the saddle bag on the donkey's back? That way you won't have the work of carrying it yourself."

"Have a fear of God, man!" Juha retorted. "Isn't it enough that I'm riding this poor donkey? Do you want me to tire it out carrying the saddle bag too?"

Juha was digging in the ground outside the city of Kufa, and an acquaintance of his passed by.

"What's the matter, Juha?" the man asked. "Why are you digging?"

"I buried some money here in the desert," Juha said, "but I can't find the spot."

"Well," said the other man, "you should have marked it."

"I did," replied Juha. "It was right in the shade of a cloud up there in the sky. And now the shade's completely gone."

❧

Two imbeciles were walking along a road. "Let's each make a wish," one of them said.

The first man said he wished he had a thousand sheep, and the second said he wished he had a thousand wolves.

"Why's that?" asked the first man.

"So my wolves can eat your sheep," answered the second.

The first man, furious, began heaping abuse on the second, who gave as good as he got in return, until finally they came to blows.

At this point Juha happened to pass by, with two jars of honey on the back of his donkey, and he asked what the matter was. When they told him, he unloaded the two jars of honey and spilled their contents out on the ground.

"May God," he said, "shed my blood as I've spilled this honey, if you aren't a pair of imbeciles!"

❧

Juha entered the palace of a city dignitary, along with a good number of notables who were discussing various weighty matters. They noticed, though, that Juha remained silent.

"What are you thinking about?" they asked him.

"I'm just wondering," he replied, "how such a great big table got through this little door!"

❧

His mother went to a wedding, leaving him instructions to guard the door. So, he sat with his back against the door, until finally it struck him his mother had been away much longer than he'd expected. So, he unscrewed the door from its hinges, hoisted it onto his back and carried it off to where his mother was.

She saw him and asked him what he was doing.

"Well," he said, "you told me to guard the door. Here it is—I've kept it safe."

❧

Juha was searching for his lost donkey, muttering the whole time, "Praise be to God!"

"Why do you keep saying that?" people asked him.

"I'm praising God I wasn't riding my donkey," he said. "If I had been, I would have been lost too."

❧

Juha bought two pigeons for eleven piasters. As he was heading home with the pigeons in his hands, a friend met him and asked how much they'd cost. Rather than use words to tell him, Juha opened his hands to show the price with his fingers—and off flew the two pigeons.

Juha went on a long journey with a pumpkin tied around his neck—so, he said, it wouldn't get lost. When he reached a village and fell asleep there, a man came along, took the pumpkin and tied it around his own neck. Juha woke and saw the man. "Amazing!" he said. "That man's me. So who am I?"

Juha went to fetch water from the well, and there he saw the reflection of the moon gazing up at him. Thinking the moon must have fallen in the well, he decided he ought to save it. So, he brought a rope with a hook he'd attached to the end and threw it down into the well. The hook caught on a big stone, and Juha started pulling and pulling, so hard that the rope flew off and Juha fell flat on his back. Then he saw the moon up in the sky.

"I've put myself to a lot of trouble," he thought. "Still, I've saved the poor thing from drowning."

The lamp flickered out in the dead of night, and his wife asked him to pass her the matches that were on his left.

"Are you crazy, woman?" he retorted. "How do you expect me to know my right from my left when it's pitch dark like this?"

"Which is more useful," someone asked Juha, "the sun or the moon?"

He didn't hesitate for a moment.

"The moon," he answered firmly. "No question about it."

"Why's that?" they asked.

"Because," he answered, "the sun rises during the day, when you don't need it. But the moon comes out in the dark. And that's when you need it."

One day, Juha was asked about the remedy for a bad eye.

"I had a painful toothache once," he said. "And the only way I found of easing the pain was to have it taken out."

His wife was in some pain and asked him to fetch the doctor to her. But by the time he'd got ready and was leaving the house, her pain had gone. So, she shouted to him from a window that there wasn't any more need for a doctor. He, though, hurried on his way.

"My wife," he told the doctor, when he'd arrived, "felt some pain and asked me to fetch you. Then she told me from the window the pain had gone, and you weren't needed any more. That's why I came to find you—to tell you that you needn't bother to come now."

Juha went to a grocer and bought ten piasters' worth of oil, which the grocer started pouring into a container Juha had brought with him. But the container wasn't big enough to hold all the oil he'd bought, so he turned it upside down (letting the oil flow out) for the grocer to pour in the rest. On his way home, a man he met asked him how much he'd paid for the oil.

"Ten piasters," Juha said.

"What?" the man said. "For that little amount?"

Juha turned the container upside down.

"No," he said. "I got all this too."

Juha handed his manservant a jar to fill with water from the river, then gave him a mighty slap in the face, warning him not to break the jar.

"Why did you slap him," someone asked, "when he hadn't broken the jar?"

"I wanted," Juha answered, "to show him what he'd get if he was careless. He'll take proper care now."

One day a neighbor asked him if he had any vinegar that was forty years old.

"I do indeed," Juha said.

The neighbor asked him for a little of it, but Juha said he couldn't give him any. The neighbor inquired why.

"If I agreed," Juha said, "and did the same with everyone else who asked, how would I have any vinegar that was forty years old?"

⁂

Someone complained to Juha that the inside of his house never saw the sun. Juha asked him if the sun visited his farm, and the man confirmed that it did.

"In that case," Juha said, "move your house to your farm."

⁂

It was the custom of the Anatolians to allocate tasks on a teamwork basis—one person would do a job for several or even many others. One such task involved the grinding of wheat and other grains. Rather than have everyone go to the mill, which was several hours' journey away, a single person would drive a caravan of donkeys there, loaded with many neighbors' crops.

When it was Juha's turn to carry the crops to the mill, he took charge of eight of his neighbors' donkeys, each with its load of wheat, mounted his own donkey and started off. After he'd gone some way, it occurred to him to count the donkeys; but he didn't count his own, which he was still riding. He found, accordingly, that he only had eight donkeys, and became almost frantic, worrying where his own donkey was. He dismounted, and he looked behind the trees and around various bends, but he couldn't find any donkey there. So, he went back to the caravan, counted the donkeys from where he was standing, and found there were nine. Praising God, he got up on his donkey and carried on with his journey.

After a little while, he started worrying all over again. So, he counted the donkeys while still riding his own, and found there were only eight. Perplexed, he pondered for a good while. Then he got down and counted the donkeys once more. When he found there were nine, he grew quite distraught, his mind darkened by thoughts of the tricks of jinn and devils. He started reciting verses from the Holy Quran, then got up on his donkey and carried on with his journey.

Yet again he was gripped by ugly suspicions, and he counted the donkeys, only to find the number was back down to eight. He dismounted and started shouting at the top of his voice, reciting verses from the Holy Quran and beseeching God's help. He began, in his fright, to hear strange voices, and he started shaking like the leaves of a tree in a strong wind. He tried to unload the donkeys, but couldn't manage it, and so he cowered in a corner, quite exhausted, waiting for someone to pass who might bring him some comfort.

After not too long a man came by and saw Shaikh Juha in this state—and everyone knew well enough about Shaikh Juha and his states! He asked what had happened, and Juha told his story.

"As if I didn't have enough problems with human beings," Juha went on, "now jinn and devils want to make fun of me!"

"It's not that way at all," the man told him. "It's just a delusion that's taken hold of you. You haven't seen anything, have you?"

Indeed, Juha said, he hadn't seen anything, but he'd heard some disturbing noises. The man kept him company and, after they'd had something to eat,

Juha's mood improved: he livened up and started leaping playfully around. Then he mounted his donkey and said goodbye to the man.

Still, he told himself, he might as well count the donkeys. And, when he did, he found there were eight. He yelled out to the man.

"Look!" he said, his voice thick with tears. "There are still only eight. What is this fearful thing that's happened to me?"

The man hesitated slightly. Then he asked Juha if he'd counted the donkey he was riding. Surely that must be where the problem over numbers had sprung from.

Juha struck his brow with the palm of his hand, dismounted and bent over the man's hands, kissing them in gratitude.

"May God," he said, "bless you! You've put me right, and made me feel calm and easy in my mind again! I nearly went mad over what was happening to me. There are so many events that fling man into the cradle of puzzlement and perplexity. All human disasters spring from the mind failing to grasp the truth, through some chance mental block. Then, when the realm of truth opens up, it becomes clear to all. When truth's revealed like that, then enemies embrace, all hatred and contention vanishes between them, and they live their lives in happiness!"

✿✾

He was taking along ten donkeys and riding one of them. It occurred to him to count them, and he found there were only nine. So, he got down and started looking for the tenth donkey. Then, before he re-mounted, he counted them again and found there were ten.

"I'd do better," he said to himself, "to walk and gain a donkey than ride and lose one."

⁂

Juha's town was visited by a renowned scholar, who inquired whether there were any scholars there. The townsfolk named Juha and took the visitor to him.

When they met, the visiting scholar said: "I have forty questions. Can you give one single answer for all of them?"

"Yes," Juha answered. "Let me hear your questions."

The visiting scholar rolled out his forty questions.

"And," Juha said, "you want one single answer— to cover all of those?"

"That's precisely what I'm looking for," the visitor stated.

"Well," Juha replied, "there's nothing so very difficult about that. I can't answer any of them."

⁂

Juha came across a stranger in the street. Still, he addressed the man, and, after a few exchanges, dropped all formality and started talking at length.

The man was surprised.

"Do you know me?" he asked. "What makes you think you can talk in that free and easy way?"

"For a moment," Juha said, "I thought you were me, because you're dressed like me and you walk in the same kind of way. But I see now we're not the same person."

Juha was trying vainly to sell a cow he had. A broker in the marketplace saw him and offered to sell it for the usual fee. Juha agreed, and the merchant promptly started crying out details of the cow, noting all its various uses and good qualities, including the fact that it was six months pregnant. The cow was swiftly sold.

Some time after, matchmakers came to Juha's house to ask for his daughter's hand in marriage to a particular suitor. As they were expanding on his daughter's good qualities, he remembered the one that had led his cow to be sold so quickly.

"She's everything you see, and more," he told the matchmakers. "On top of everything else, she's six months pregnant!"

❧

Juha had some fruit in his kerchief.

"What's that in your kerchief, Juha?" someone asked him.

"I'm not telling you," he said. "But I'll give you the biggest plum if you can guess what's there."

"They're plums, aren't they?" said the man who'd asked.

"What cursed wretch told you that," Juha asked angrily, "when they're all tied up in a kerchief?"

❧

Someone wanted to test Juha.

"If you can guess what's in my kerchief," he said, "I'll give you something to make a lovely omelet with."

"Now what could that be?" Juha said. "Describe it, will you?"

"It's white on the outside and yellow on the inside," the friend said.

"I know!" Juha said. "It's a turnip stuffed with carrots!"

❧

It was Juha's habit, when he fasted during Ramadan, to throw a pebble in a jar for every day gone by. His daughter saw him doing this, and, thinking to be helpful, tossed in two handfuls of pebbles.

"How many more days are there in Ramadan?" his neighbors asked him one day.

"I don't know how many there are left," he said, "but I can tell you how many have gone."

With that he counted the pebbles and found there were more than 120.

"If I tell them 120," he thought to himself, "they'll just laugh at me. I'll bring it down to forty."

So, out he went to them and said: "We've had around forty days of the month."

They all started laughing at him. But he only laughed right back.

"Ramadan seems to go on for ever when you're fasting," he told them. "Just what would you have said, I wonder, if I'd told you the real number?"

❧

People saw Juha searching on the ground, and yet there was nothing there.

"What are you looking for?" they asked him.

"A ring's fallen off my finger," he told them.

"Well, how can it have dropped here?" they asked. "There's no sign of anything."

"Well, actually," he said, "it fell off in that alley over there."

"So why don't you look for it there?" they asked him. "Where you dropped it?"

"What's the use of that?" he said. "It's dark in there."

❧

Juha was part owner of a house. So, he sold the half he owned to buy the half he didn't own. That way, he thought, he'd be the owner of the whole house, and have no one to share with.

❧

One day people heard him running along and singing.

"What's all this about?" they asked him. "This running and singing?"

"I like to listen to my own voice from a distance," he told them.

❧

"Why," someone asked Juha, "are people scattered over every corner of the earth? And why do they go this way and that way every morning?"

He thought for a while.

"Well," he said at last, "if they all moved in the same direction, the earth would tilt with their weight, and they'd drop into a bottomless pit."

One day Juha went to the public bath, where he found things very quiet. So, he started singing, relishing the sound he was making. Blessed with such a wondrous voice, he told himself, surely he ought not to withhold his gift from his Muslim brothers. And so, when he left the bath, he headed straight for the mosque, and, when the call to noon prayer was sounded, climbed the minaret and started chanting songs to the glory of God.

Those passing by were amazed—in fact his voice was gratingly harsh and unmelodious. "What do you think you're doing, you imbecile?" one of them said. "Why are you getting on everyone's nerves, chanting in that fearful voice of yours? At this of all hours?"

"Brother," Juha answered, from the top of the minaret, "if some charitable person would like to build me a bath, up here on top of this minaret, I'll chant with such a voice you'll forget the singing of nightingales!"

Juha dreamed that someone owed him ten dinars but had only paid him back nine. He demanded his money, but they couldn't agree and started quarreling about it. At the height of the quarrel, Juha started out of his sleep, and found, in his fright, that his hand was empty. Distraught now, he started reproaching himself for his greed. Then he lay back down on his bed, thrust his head under the covers, and stretched out his hand to the phantom opponent.

"All right," he said. "No need to get worked up. Just give me the nine!"

One day Juha appeared dressed in black.

"Why are you wearing black like that?" an acquaintance asked him. "Has something terrible happened?"

"Yes," Juha answered. "My son's father died."

※

One day Juha was preaching.

"You Muslims!" he said. "Give praise to God for not creating camels with wings. If they could fly, they'd land on the roofs of your houses and bring them down over your heads!"

※

One day Juha was preaching in a strange town.

"You Muslims!" he said. "I see the air in this town is just like the air in ours."

"How do you work that out?" the others asked.

"The number of stars up in your sky," he answered, "and the shape of the stars—they're just the same as they are in our sky at Aaq Shahr. So it's obvious, isn't it, that our air's like yours?"

※

Juha had a hen that died, leaving several young chicks. So, Juha took some black ribbons and tied them around the chicks' heads.

"Why did you do that, Juha?" he was asked.

"It's in mourning for their late mother," he said.

"They're receiving condolences."

❧

He was walking down the street, and a thorn stuck painfully in his foot. When he got home, he took it out, then said: "The Lord be praised!"

"What makes you praise God?" his wife asked.

"I'm praising Him," Juha replied, "because I wasn't wearing my new shoes. The thorn would have made a hole in one of them."

❧

Juha wanted to sell his donkey, so he headed for the market. On the way, he went across a muddy spot, and the donkey's tail became daubed with mud. He couldn't, he reckoned, sell the donkey with mud all over its tail, so he cut off the tail and put it in his saddle bag. When he reached the market, people gathered around him.

"What a fine donkey that is," they said. "Such a pity it doesn't have a tail!"

"Let's agree the price first," Juha said. "The tail isn't far away. It's right here in the saddle bag. Whoever buys the donkey can have it."

❧

He took his donkey to the market. A buyer approached and opened the donkey's mouth to see how old it was, whereupon the donkey gave his hand a nasty bite. The man let out a flurry of curses and abuse, and marched angrily off.

Then another buyer came up and circled the donkey. He went to feel the tail, and the donkey gave him a vicious kick, knocking him to the ground. The man got up, mouthing insults and curses, and went off.

At this point the broker came up to Juha.

"Let me tell you," he said, "no one's going to buy a donkey that bites and kicks like that."

"I didn't bring it here to sell," Juha replied. "I brought it so all my Muslim brothers could see how much grief it causes me!"

. 5 .

Juha the Butt

Once Juha was deeply in debt, and his case was brought before the governor, who bore him ill will—Juha was constantly exposing the man's shortcomings and unjust rulings, and so provoking people against him. The vainglorious governor now had the chance to take his revenge. Knowing Juha to be short of money, he gave orders that Juha should be carried around the town on a mule, with boys shouting behind him: "This is the man who put off his creditors and didn't pay people what he owed them!"

At the end of the day, with the sentence duly carried out, Juha was returned to his house and the boys were disbanded. The muleteer approached him.

"And where, our master shaikh," he asked, "is the mule's fee for the day?"

"Woe to all stupid people!" Juha retorted. "And to wise men too! Why do you think, you fool, people have been shouting like this all day long? And what was all this grand procession for?"

❧

Juha sent his son to the marketplace to buy him a grilled sheep's head. The son did this, but the appetizing smell of the meat was too much for him, and he ate the ears, then the eyes and tongue and brain. Finally he went back to his father.

"And where," Juha inquired, "are its eyes?"

"It was blind," his son answered.

"Well, where are its ears?" Juha asked.

"It was deaf," came the answer.

"So, where's its tongue?" Juha asked.

"It was dumb," the son replied.

"And where's its brain gone?" Juha persisted.

"It didn't have one," was the answer. "It was a teacher of small boys."

So, Juha told his son to take the head back to the seller.

"I can't," said the son. "I bought it 'as is'."

⁂

Juha came to a village where, so he'd heard, the people were very miserly. He wanted to test this out for himself, so he went up to one of them, asked for a drink and was given a bowl full of milk.

"I'd heard, brother," he said, having drunk the milk and thanked the man for his kindness, "that you were all stingy and miserly here. And yet I've found you to be generous. You didn't just give me water, you gave me milk."

"I wouldn't have given it to you," the man answered. "Only, a mouse had fallen in it."

Juha, furious, flung the bowl down on the ground.

"Careful!" the man yelled. "Don't break that bowl! It's the one my daughter uses to piddle in!"

⁂

He was traveling in a group of people, and they all stopped for a rest. When they went to resume their journey, he put his right foot in the left-hand stirrup, and, jumping up, found himself mounted backwards. Everyone laughed at him.

"What are you laughing at?" he asked. "Just because my mule's put its head to the back and its buttocks to the front!"

༺༻

Juha went to the market to buy the things he needed, then summoned a porter to carry them all, generously paying him his fee in advance. When, though, Juha's attention was distracted, the rascally porter made off with the goods.

Juha went around asking people to help, but everyone just made fun of him. He was, they said, absent-minded and stupid. They all paid tribute to the porter for the cunning way he'd behaved—not a single person blamed him or helped Juha look for him.

Ten days later, though, a friend of his took him aside and told him where he could find the porter. Juha promptly started running off.

"What's this, Shaikh Juha?" his friends asked disdainfully. "You're letting a thief get away with your goods?"

"Leave well alone, you people!" Juha said. "The thief's been gone ten days now. I'm afraid he'll demand a fee for all ten of them! By God, if he did that in front of you, here in your town, I reckon you'd all stand up for him."

. 6 .

Boastfulness and False Pride

Juha was in the habit of exaggerating things. "Let's make a bargain," one of his friends told him. "If I find you exaggerating in anything you say, I'll say 'ahem' to warn you."

One day Juha was talking to some people.

"I built a mosque in town," he told them, "and it was a thousand meters long."

A prompt "ahem" came from his friend. Juha said nothing.

"And how wide was it?" someone asked.

"One meter," Juha answered.

His hearers were surprised at this. "Why did you make it so narrow?" they asked.

Juha looked at his friend.

"What can we do?" he asked. "Other people have forced us to make it narrow. May God make things narrow for them!"

❧

A number of people, Juha among them, were sitting around boasting of their horsemanship.

"One day," Juha said, "people brought along a mettlesome stallion. One horseman tried to approach it, but he didn't manage it. Then another one tried to jump up and mount, and got a kick for his pains. Then a third had a try, but the stallion wouldn't give an inch. The challenge appealed to me. I rolled up my sleeves, gathered the edges of my robe around me, grabbed hold of the horse's mane, leapt up—"

At this point another person, who knew Juha well, broke in.

"And fell off," he said.

❧

Juha sat in a coffee house, bragging how much gold and money he had. A thief overheard him and coveted his wealth, and so he waited for night to fall, then went to Juha's house to rob him. He searched through every room, but, finding nothing worth stealing, he lost his temper completely and stood there damning and cursing Juha. Then, as he was making to leave, he found Juha standing by the door. He looked sheepish, but Juha gave him a gracious welcome.

The thief made no reply, moving toward the door and looking to make good his escape.

"Shut the door, won't you," Juha said, "so thieves can't get in and steal all our gold and money?"

This was too much for the thief.

"Curse you, Juha!" he snapped. "It was that sort of talk that lured me here in the first place!"

❧

Juha bought eggs at nine for a dirham, then sold them at ten for a dirham.

"Why are you selling at a loss, Juha?" the others asked him.

"All I'm concerned about," he said, "is for people to say I'm a merchant. I want my friends to see me buying and selling!"

One day Juha wanted to ride a horse. He leapt up, but couldn't mount it.

"Oh, if I could only be young again!" he cried.

Then, looking around, he saw there was no one there.

"Actually," he admitted, "I wasn't any better then than I am now."

Juha was riding his mule, and he fell off with his foot caught in the stirrup. A number of youths saw him and started making fun of him.

"Juha's fallen off his mule!" they cried.

"Don't you lads laugh!" he said. "I'd just decided to get off anyway."

He claimed he was a saint.

"So," they said, "what miracles can you perform?"

"Believe me," he said, "I can tell trees to come and they obey me."

"All right then," they said. "Tell that palm tree to come to you."

"Oh palm tree," he said, "come to me!" He repeated this three times, but it didn't come. With that he got up and started walking.

"Where are you going, Juha?" they asked him.

"Prophets and saints," he told them, "are free of all arrogance or vanity. If the palm tree won't come to me, then I'll go to the palm tree!"

A certain person claimed he was a saint and could perform miracles.

"Don't you have anything to do in life," he asked Juha, "except babble and play around? Can you perform miracles? If you can, let's see them."

"Can you perform miracles?" Juha asked him.

"Every night," the man said, "I fly and ascend to heaven."

"And do you," Juha asked, "feel something as soft as a fan touching your face?"

"Indeed I do," said the man.

"Well," Juha said, "what you can feel is the long ear of the donkey I'm riding."

. 7 .

A Witty Rogue

The city where Juha lived had a drunkard for a judge. One day the judge went to a nearby orchard, got dead drunk and put his turban and cloak to one side. Juha, who was out walking, came upon the judge, snatched the cloak, put it on and walked off.

Eventually the judge sobered up and missed the cloak and he gave the court clerk the task of finding it and bringing in the thief. The clerk searched around, and, finding Juha wearing it, took him off to the judge, who asked him how he'd come by that particular cloak.

"Yesterday," Juha said, "I went to an orchard with some friends, and we stumbled on a drunk who was sleeping it off. He was in the most appalling state. So, I took his cloak and put it on. I can produce witnesses to support this, and they'll tell you and everyone else who this drunkard was."

"We're not interested," the judge said, "in the identity of this worthless person. Wear the cloak to your heart's desire. I want nothing to do with the owner."

❧

Juha's town had a judge who was notorious for taking bribes. One day, Juha had a contract that needed his endorsement. So, Juha presented the judge with a large jar that, he said, contained honey.

When the judge learned of this, he went into the guest room, welcomed Juha warmly and sealed the contract with the necessary endorsement. Juha then threw the judge a meaningful look, took the contract and left.

A few days later someone presented the judge with some cream, and he hurried off with this to the jar of honey to enjoy some honey and cream. He dipped the spoon into the honey jar—and out came a piece of mud dried on the bottom.

Furious, the judge instructed his clerk to go and summon Juha. The clerk approached Juha respectfully.

"Sir," he said, "an error has occurred in the composition and cross-referencing in respect of the endorsement of the contract. Your brother, the judge, would like to rectify this error, then return the contract to you."

Juha smiled sarcastically.

"There's no flaw in the contract," he said. "Any flaw just happens to be in the mind of our master, the judge. I pray God to rectify it for him."

֍

A wealthy man told Juha: "If you'll go and spit in the face of my enemy, I'll give you a sum of money."

Juha agreed, walked up to the man and spat in his face. The man thereupon took Juha in front of the judge, who questioned Juha, only to be told, "I have a decree authorizing me to do this."

The judge told Juha to show him the decree, and Juha passed to the judge a pouch containing half the sum he'd received from his wealthy friend. The judge took the pouch, then promptly addressed the claimant.

"Your opponent," he told the man, "has indeed produced a decree authorizing him to spit in your face. In anyone's face, come to that—even mine."

❧

Juha was a judge and quite ready to take bribes.

"I was sitting at home once," he said, "when someone came and told me about a case he had against a particular person. He made a claim that I found quite plausible. Then he said: 'Sir, you're our head and our judge, and I've appraised you of my case. Clearly, I have right on my side.' 'Brother,' I told him, 'you have right fully on your side.'

"The man had hardly left when his opponent arrived. He greeted me and recounted the case in all its detail, making, in the course of this, a claim which I found quite plausible. 'This, our esteemed judge,' he concluded, 'is my case, and, clearly, I have right fully on my side.'

"'Brother,' I told him, 'you do indeed have right fully on your side.'

"My wife, seeing and hearing all this, got angry and upset at the whole thing.

"'How can this be right, Juha?' she asked. 'Is your eminence a judge or simply two-faced? How can both the opponents have right on their side, in one and the same case?'

"This accursed wife of mine knew well enough that the first man had brought a jar of ghee to our house, while the second man had brought us a jar of honey. And as long as there's ghee and honey, then everyone's in the right, whether the right likes it or not! By the very nature of the case, the two opponents are respectively in the right.

"But women simply don't let up, and, as everyone knows, they won't stop talking. I didn't want to launch into an argument with my wife, in case someone heard us and let the cat out of the bag. So I gave way.

"'Indeed, my dear wife,' I told her, 'you too have right fully on your side!'"

※※※

[The governor Kameesh was the living embodiment of the corruption of justice and the judiciary in his time. Clever though he was, and full of mental agility, he was driven by greed and avarice. He had no compunction about cutting corners, and no shame about fabricating feeble justifications only the most stupid or naïve person would ever dream of. This is demonstrated in the following anecdote.]

One day the governor was walking around, inspecting the city streets, when he sniffed the mouth-watering smell of grilling coming from a bakery nearby. He summoned the baker and a puerile argument ensued, which ended with the governor ordering the baker to send the grilled goose to his house, and to tell the real owner that it had flown off after being cooked.

"If the owner isn't satisfied," the governor concluded, "then come straight to me and I'll judge between the two of you. I'll deal with him, don't worry."

The baker gave in to the governor and sent the goose to his house. When the owner of the goose arrived to claim it, and the baker told him it had flown off, he was furious. The two of them started quarreling, and people nearby sided with the customer, saying the baker was a thief. They kept on at him, until, in the end, he became desperate, panicked, and ran off like a madman, having first given the nearest man such a vicious punch that it knocked out one of his teeth.

The mob's mood grew uglier, but the desperate baker managed to leap into a nearby alley, where he found his path blocked by a pregnant woman returning home with her husband. He gave her such a kick that she lost the child. The mob, angrier still, kept following him, but off he shot like an arrow from a bow, entered a nearby mosque and climbed to the top of the minaret. The mob still followed in hot pursuit, and so he jumped from the top of the minaret and landed on one of his pursuers. The man died but the baker survived. As the mob's anger grew fiercer still, the baker fled into a butcher's shop, where he seized hold of a knife, pretending to be crazy.

Now, Juha's donkey was nearby, and, as the baker slashed downward with the knife, he cut off the donkey's tail. Then he ran off to the residence of the governor Kameesh, the mob still pursuing. Finally they all fetched up in the governor's presence.

Kameesh, for his part, feigned surprise and pretended to have no knowledge of the baker. Then, having heard the full story, he told everyone he believed the baker's claim: that the goose had flown off after being grilled, so demonstrating the power of the Creator, praise be to Him. The goose's owner grew furious at this, whereupon Kameesh, in his capacity as judge, accused him of heresy and lack of faith in the Creator's power, fining him ten dinars accordingly.

The governor then addressed the case of the second plaintiff, who was instructed to strike the baker a single blow that would knock out exactly the same tooth as the one he'd lost—and woe betide him if it was otherwise! The man, realizing how biased the judge was, and despairing of justice, relinquished his case. The governor thereupon fined him ten dinars.

Next it was the turn of the third opponent. "The fault," the judge told him, "lies with your late brother. Why did he have to choose that precise moment to walk under the minaret? Still, let right prevail and justice take its course. You must climb the selfsame minaret and jump down on top of the baker, killing him as he did, indeed, kill your brother." The claimant, realizing the judge's perversity and despairing of justice at his hands, relinquished his right, and the judge ruled he should be fined ten dinars for failing to carry out the decision of the court.

Now it was the turn of the woman who'd lost her child. The judge admonished her for choosing to pass, at that very moment, along a street she knew to be narrow—though in fact (he went on) the real fault lay with her husband, who'd arranged for her to live in such a street. But, be that as it may, justice must take its course. He decreed, accordingly, that the one who'd caused the abortion in her womb must make it pregnant again in lieu. The woman and her husband were stunned, and she relinquished her right. The judge imposed a fine of ten dinars on her for wasting the court's time.

Juha, having witnessed the awesome judgments of this crazed tyrant, fled with his donkey, looking only to make good his escape. The governor, though, forestalled him, whereupon Juha cried out that God had created his donkey without either tail or brains. This the governor, egged on by the baker, refused to accept, and Juha saw it was useless to argue with him. He gazed at the governor.

"My lord governor," Juha said, "so it is. God created my donkey without either tail or brains. Are you denying the might of the Creator? Do you doubt and contend His power?"

The governor, hearing his own reasoning thrown back at him, was dumbstruck and found no reply.

৵৵

Juha had a crow that settled on the horn of a buffalo, and deciding the buffalo was a fair spoil of the hunt, he took it off with him. Then, though, he realized the buffalo belonged to a neighbor of his, and this neighbor submitted the matter to a corrupt judge, demanding that his buffalo be returned. But Juha presented the judge, by way of a bribe, with a jar supposed to be filled with ghee, and the judge ruled that the buffalo belonged to Juha.

Soon the judge discovered the jar was filled with animal droppings and, determined to take his revenge, he summoned Juha to appear in front of him. Juha, though, had a surprise in store.

"Did you ever hear," he asked, "of a lame crow worth just two piasters subduing, in a hunt, the head of a buffalo worth a thousand piasters? How did you decide the buffalo belonged to me? On what body of law was this decision based?"

The corrupt judge was taken aback by this and, from that day on, exerted himself to decide justly and refuse bribes. As for Juha, the cause of the judge's repentance, he in turn returned the buffalo to its rightful owner.

৵৵

A common citizen came to Juha (then a judge) and complained that one of the town's notables had struck him and bitten his ear. The claimant demanded due reprisal in the name of justice and equity. Juha summoned the notable and, with great courtesy and respect, inquired as to the facts of the commoner's claim. The notable answered, with casual indifference, that the claimant had in fact bitten his own ear.

Juha, pondering the matter, found himself in a quandary. The claim was clearly justified. Yet how could he possibly accept the claim of a pauper with no social status? Finally he decided to conduct an experiment on himself: he adjourned the court, went home, and there made an attempt to bite his own ear. He tried it in various positions, but all in vain, and finally he fell over and cracked his head.

He had his head dressed and went back to court, where the claimant approached him demanding a ruling in his favor. Juha was, he said, judge among Muslims and the leader of those vindicating victims of injustice. How, after all, could a man bite his own ear?

"Indeed, my son," Juha said, "a man can bite his own ear, then fall over and crack his head on the floor, and break various other parts of his body too. You ought to praise God that all you did was bite your own ear. Otherwise you would have met the same fate I did!"

❧

"Come with me to court," someone said to Juha, "and testify that I lent a hundred stones of wheat. I'll give you twenty dinars if you do."

Juha pocketed the money and went off to court with the man. There, before the judge, the man made his claim, that he'd lent the person in question a hundred stones of wheat, and the judge asked whether there were any witnesses.

"Juha will testify for me," the man said.

The judge addressed Juha.

"Do you testify to this effect?" he asked.

"Sir," Juha answered, "I testify this man lent the other man a hundred stones of barley."

"He claims," the judge observed, "that it was wheat. Now you're saying it was barley!"

"Sir," Juha responded, "since the whole claim's unfounded anyway, and my evidence is fraudulent, then wheat and barley come to much the same thing."

❧

A miller saw Juha taking stuff from other people's baskets and putting it in his own.

"What do you think you're doing, Juha?" he yelled.

"Don't be hard on me," Juha said. "I'm just stupid, that's all."

"If you really were stupid," the miller said, "wouldn't you be taking stuff out of your own basket and putting it in other people's?"

"What are you saying?" Juha rejoined. "I'm only one idiot. If I acted like that, I'd be two idiots in one!"

One day Juha went into an orchard when the owner wasn't there, and started picking all the fruit and vegetables he could lay his hands on, until finally he'd filled his bag with them. Just as he was leaving, he saw, to his panic and confusion, that the gardener was coming back.

"What are you doing in here?" the gardener demanded.

"That storm that blew up yesterday," he somehow managed to say, "it took hold of me and dumped me down here. I didn't have any choice."

"In that case," the gardener said, "who picked all that stuff in your bag?"

"The wind was so strong," Juha said, "it tossed me about, here, there and everywhere. I'd grab for a hold, but the vegetables and fruit just kept coming away, and they stayed there, gripped in my hands."

"Well, all right then," the gardener said, "who put all the stuff in the bag, until it was stuffed right to the top?"

Juha was nonplussed this time.

"I've been wondering about that too," he said at last. "And the plain fact is, seeing you here drove the answer clean out of my mind."

One day Juha traveled to Konya and went into a confectioner's shop, where there were all kinds of tempting sweetmeats on display. He went up to one of these.

"In the name of God!" he said. And with that he

started gobbling down the things on the plate, one after the other.

"What do you think you're doing," the pastry-cook demanded, "just strolling in and eating other people's property like that?"

Juha, though, paid no attention. He just went on eating. The shopkeeper picked up a stick and started beating him with it, but Juha only kept eating faster still.

"God bless you people of Konya!" he said. "You actually beat your guests, to force them to eat your sweets."

. 8 .

Cowardice

Juha married a woman who was very fat, and he was afraid she'd be too strong for him and do him harm. One day, when she was chasing after him with a cane in her hand, he hid under the bed, where she was too fat to follow him.

"Come here after me," he yelled, feeling safe at last. "If you're man enough!"

◈

"I heard the most extraordinary yelling and din in your house," a neighbor told him. "It sounded like a quarrel, and then as if something went clattering down the stairs."

"Well," Juha said, "there was a bit of a quarrel between me and my wife. She hit my cloak, and it fell on the floor, then clattered down the stairs. That's what made all the noise."

But how, his neighbor inquired, could a cloak make such a noise?

"Brother," Juha answered, "don't be so fussy over every little detail. I was inside the cloak!"

◈

Juha was a cowardly fellow. Yet every day he'd tell his wife the most monstrous lies, spinning her fantastic tales about how brave and strong he was. His wife (who knew he was afraid of his own shadow) finally decided she'd had enough.

Each day he'd buy a long staff, stain it with blood, then claim he'd used it to kill robbers who'd attacked him while he was walking at night. One day his wife hid aside from the street, then, when he got close to her, coughed loudly.

Juha, terrified, flung away his staff and ran off, whereupon his jubilant wife picked it up, then got back to the house before him. After a while, in Juha came, gasping for breath, his mouth dry as a kiln.

"Why are you in such a state?" she asked him.

"Forty thieves," he answered, "pounced on me in the dark, while I was walking along. I killed them all with my staff."

"So, where's your staff now?" she inquired.

"It broke over their heads," Juha said. "It was no use anymore, so I threw it away."

She got up and went to fetch the staff.

"Here it is," she said. "All in one piece. I found it out on the road and brought it back for you. But, when I got home, I found the forty thieves you killed had been brought back to life, and they've come to your house to rob you, to get their own back."

"Where are the robbers then?" Juha asked.

"They're hiding under the stairs," his wife answered. "Go and rout them out and kill them."

Juha went off to bed and wrapped himself in the covers.

"You go and deal with them yourself," he told her. "I could never kill someone God's brought back to life!"

Juha was traveling, armed with a sword and a musket. A man carrying a club met with him on the road and robbed him of everything he had—he even took Juha's donkey and clothes. Juha went back to his town in this state.

"What happened to you, Juha?" they asked. He told them the whole story.

"Oh Juha!" they said then. "How could someone on foot, carrying a club, rob someone who was riding a donkey and had a sword and a musket?"

"One of my hands," he said, "was taken up with the sword, and the other one was taken up with my musket. What was I supposed to do while he was robbing me—hit him with my teeth? But let me tell you, I gave him as bad a fright as he gave me."

"What did you do?" they asked. "How did you frighten him?"

"After he'd gone around a mile," Juha said, "I yelled the most fearsome insults at him. There wasn't a curse under the sun I didn't use!"

. 9 .

Justice and Generosity

W hen someone asks you for something," Juha was asked, "why is it you don't give it until the next day?"

"I do that," he answered, "so they'll appreciate the value of whatever it is I'm giving."

❧

Once, when Juha had been appointed a judge, a cook complained to him how a poor man had found a dry morsel of bread, then passed it over the steam of the food he was cooking and eaten it. The cook demanded the price of the steam.

Juha took out a bag of coins and counted them, making them jingle as he did it.

"You can take the jingling of the coins," he told the cook, "as the price for the flavorsome steam of your cooking."

❧

When Juha was sitting as a judge, a cunning person came to him and claimed he was owed a sum of money by a certain woodcutter. This, he said, was because he'd cheered the woodcutter on, shouting "hela, hop!" again and again, while the man was doing his work. This had made it easier to cut the wood.

"And how much," Juha asked, "do you intend to charge him for this assistance of yours?"

"Five dirhams," answered the man.

Juha accordingly took five dirhams from his money bag and struck them against one another, making them ring.

"Now you've heard the five dirhams ringing," he told the sly claimant. "Take that as your fee—one encouraging sound for another."

❧

Two men, unable to settle their dispute, took their differences to Judge Juha.

"This man," the claimant said, "was carrying a heavy load, and it fell off his shoulders. He asked me to help him. When I asked him how much he'd pay me, he said, 'nothing,' and I agreed to this. Now I want him to pay me my nothing."

"Your claim's a fair one, my son," Juha told him. "Come here, to me, and lift this book."

The claimant did so, and Juha asked him what he'd found underneath the book.

"Nothing," replied the claimant.

"Very well," Juha admonished him. "Now, take it and be off with you."

❧

A thief went into a butcher's shop and ordered some meat. Then, while the butcher was busy cutting the meat, he opened the money drawer and stole some silver coins. But the butcher noticed this, grabbed him by the throat, and hauled him off in front of Judge Juha.

When he'd heard each side's story, Juha found

himself perplexed as to his judgment. So, he ordered a bowl of hot water to be brought and put the coins in it. Before too long a film of fat appeared on the surface of the water, and by this Juha knew the coins were the butcher's. He returned the man his coins and ordered the thief to be taken to prison.

❧

A man was sleeping in an orchard with his cloak over him as a cover. A thief came by and took the cloak, but the man woke, seized hold of the thief and led him in front of Judge Juha.

There before him, each man claimed the cloak was his own, and Juha was perplexed as to where the truth lay. So, he made each man hold one end of the cloak and left them like this for quite some time, while he attended to some papers. Then, suddenly, he yelled out: "You, the thief, give the cloak back to its owner!"

Taken by surprise, one of the two let go at once. Juha knew then that this man was the thief and ordered him to be imprisoned, while returning the cloak to its owner.

❧

A man killed a chicken and plucked it, then took it to the baker to grill for him, waiting at home while the task was being carried out. When the grilling was almost finished, and the delicious smell of it met the baker's nose, his avarice became too much for him, and he and his workers ate the chicken.

When the owner came to collect his bird, the baker claimed that, when the grilling was over, the chicken had turned into a beautiful princess and flown off from the bakery on its two white wings. The client, utterly dumbfounded by this, took the baker to Judge Juha, so he could make a judgment between them. Juha adjourned the case until the next day, and, in the meantime, instructed the baker to send fifty loaves of bread to his home.

Next day, both baker and customer presented themselves before Juha.

"How dare you cheat me," Juha told the baker, "by sending me charmed loaves of bread? They flew off, and, what's more, they didn't even have wings. I haven't been able to use them and I'm not paying you for them."

"But, sir," cried the astonished baker, "how can loaves fly when they don't have any wings?"

"Someone," Juha answered, "who can make a chicken turn into a girl who flies away, on her two white wings, is quite capable of making loaves fly without any wings."

෴

When Juha was a judge, a man came to him to complain he'd found his stolen mandolin with a vendor in the marketplace. When he'd tried to get it back from him, the thieving vendor had denied he'd stolen it, saying it was his own.

Juha summoned the accused vendor, then asked the mandolin's owner to bring forward his witnesses. He produced two: one of them the owner of a tavern, the other known to be lazy, brazen, and unemployed.

The two witnesses gave the same testimony: they were familiar with the mandolin, they said, and knew it belonged to the claimant. As proof of this, they attested that it had a crack in the neck and was strapped at the base. Also, its keys moved and wound loosely.

Sure enough, the description fitted the mandolin's appearance. The thief, though, asked the judge to dismiss the case, since, by law, the testimonies of a tavern owner and a lazy, brazen person were unacceptable in court.

"Yes," said Juha, "that's true enough. But when the claim's about a mandolin, then two people like that are just about the best witnesses you could have."

⬙⬙

A judge wanted to share nine geese among ten of his police officers, but was puzzled how to go about it. Some of his entourage advised him to consult Juha.

Juha set the geese in a row and lined up the police officers opposite them. Then he asked each officer to grab hold of one goose. Naturally, nine of them had a goose and the tenth was left empty-handed. This man approached Juha to ask for his share.

"Where's my goose, Juha?" he asked.

Juha wasn't disconcerted.

"The geese were right there in front of you," he told the man. "Why didn't you take one?"

. 10 .

Critic of Despotism

Juha visited the city's governor and told him he'd composed a poem in his praise; if the governor so wished, he'd recite it. The governor agreed, but, when he'd heard it, decided he didn't like it. He accordingly presented Juha with a donkey's saddle, which Juha placed on his own back, then left.

As he was leaving the palace, the governor's wife happened to meet him and asked what it was he was carrying on his shoulder.

"My lady," Juha answered, "I recited, to our lord the governor, my most splendid poem in his praise. And he presented me with his most splendid piece of clothing."

༺༻

Tamerlane was given a donkey as a present, and was quite delighted with it. Members of his entourage, seeking to flatter him, enlarged on the donkey's merits, and heaped every kind of praise on it, until finally they'd raised it to a quite extraordinary creature.

Then came Juha's turn to say something on the matter.

"I think it highly possible," he remarked, "that I could teach this donkey to read."

"If you can manage to teach it to read anything," Tamerlane said, "I'll shower you with gifts and favor. But, if you fail, I won't just brand you an imbecile, I'll have you severely punished too."

"A false claim in your presence," Juha answered, "would itself be a kind of folly or madness—and I'm no fool. Let me have enough money and allow me to stay for three months." To this Tamerlane agreed.

When the three months had passed, Juha brought the donkey into Tamerlane's court and had it stand near a chair on which he placed a huge pad. With its lips the donkey began turning the pages of the pad, one by one, and every so often looking at Juha and braying in a mournful way, as if pleading for pity. All those present were amazed, while Tamerlane, for his part, was delighted and rewarded Juha handsomely. He asked Juha how he'd managed such a feat.

"It's simple enough," Juha said. "I bought a hundred parchments of gazelle leather, marked them with lines that looked like writing, then bound them in the form of a book. I'd put barley between the pages, then turn them over, while the donkey picked up the barley a page at a time. After a while it started turning the pages on its own; and, if it forgot to do it, I'd turn the pages myself, in front of it. Finally it mastered that, so to speak. Then, in due course, I stopped putting the barley between the pages. But the donkey still kept turning the pages, looking for the barley. When it didn't find any, it brayed, in a pleading kind of way, because it was hungry."

❧

One day Tamerlane summoned the city's governor to confiscate his possessions, on the pretext that he'd stolen large quantities of funds. The truth was, the crops and fruit had been damaged that year by heaven-sent natural disasters. The previous year's harvest had indeed been plentiful, but this year the earth had produced barely enough for the people to stay alive. The governor had in fact done the best he could, using all his powers of firmness to extract everything possible from what the people had built up.

The man produced his account books, written on the paper of the day—only to see Tamerlane tear them up, then have the soldiers, on Tamerlane's orders, first flog him and then force him to eat the torn pages. Tamerlane thereupon confiscated the governor's possessions, leaving him totally destitute.

He then summoned Juha, who had a reputation for honesty, and charged him with supervision of the realm's treasury. The old man tried to wriggle out of the post, citing his failing health, but no excuse was accepted.

At the end of the month, Tamerlane called for the account books, which Juha had prepared on thin layers of bread. Tamerlane asked him just what it was he'd brought.

"Sire," Juha said, "it will end, I know, in you ordering me to swallow these. I'm an old man, not a man of fame and prowess like my predecessor. Indeed, my stomach will scarcely be able to digest even this bread!"

༺༻

Tamerlane wanted a hero to appoint to a high post in his entourage. No one, though, would agree to be put forward—for Tamerlane, as a tyrant subject to sudden changes of mood, was a thoroughly dangerous man to be close to. No one could advise Tamerlane of anyone fitted to fill the post in question.

So, the notables went to visit Juha, the man they called the savior of souls, and told him how Tamerlane held him, alone among the people of the city, in great and sincere affection. Moreover, they added, Juha knew Tamerlane's moods. He could fill the position for the moment, until they found someone to undertake it. Shaikh Juha was well-intentioned and kind-hearted, and full, too, of patriotic zeal. And so he agreed to their urgent request.

They accordingly proposed this to Tamerlane, and Tamerlane agreed. Still, he wanted to test Juha's firmness of nerve. So, he ordered Juha to stand in the middle of a field, where, on the order of the watching Tamerlane, an archer loosed an arrow between Juha's legs. The shaikh was naturally afraid, but he showed a resolute face and said nothing, mentally reciting those verses of the Holy Quran that have to do with survival. Next, a second archer was instructed to shoot an arrow that would pierce the left sleeve of Juha's robe. Again, Juha was in great fear, but still he kept up a bold appearance. Then a third archer was ordered to shoot an arrow through Juha's turban, and the knot at the top of the turban was pierced. Juha was mortally afraid now, but he stood motionless, like a concrete pillar. No physical harm had come to him, and he was congratulated on his safety and success. Aware once more of just where he was, he showed no sign of exhaustion or fear. Indeed, he started laughing.

Impressed by Juha's steadfast nerve, Tamerlane bestowed many gifts on him, including a new robe and turban. Juha thanked Tamerlane for these signs of favor. Then he said: "I beg you will order new trousers to be given me too, so as to make a full set of clothes."

"But from what we've been told," Tamerlane answered, "your trousers weren't touched. They've been inspected and found intact."

"What you've said, Sire," Juha stated, "is quite true. Your archers did the trousers no harm on the outside. But I did them such damage on the inside, myself, that I just don't know where to take hold of them now!"

⁂

"You know, don't you, Juha," Tamerlane said one day, "that each of the Abbasid caliphs had his own particular title—'Successful by the Will of God,' 'Dependent on God,' 'Taking Refuge in God,' 'Trusting in God,' and similar titles? If I'd been one of them, what title do you think I should have taken?"

"Doubtless," Juha answered at once, "Your Majesty would have been called 'It is to God that we Turn.'"

⁂

One day talk at Tamerlane's court had turned to the subject of the torments of Gehenna and the misery and torture meted out to heretics there. Juha was present, and Tamerlane addressed him.

"And where, I wonder," he said, "will we be ranked in the afterworld?"

"With the kings and great men," Juha replied, "who have left deathless names behind them."

Tamerlane was quite delighted by this.

"Which kings did you have in mind, Juha?" he asked.

Juha listed a few.

"Such as," he said, "the Pharaoh at the time of Moses, Nimrod, Hülegü, Genghis Khan—people who are like Your Majesty."

⁂

One of Tamerlane's cavalry soldiers was brought before him in a drunken state, and Tamerlane ordered he should receive eighty lashes from a cane. Juha, who was in attendance, smiled to himself, knowing as he did that this legal maximum was carried out only on those who were powerless and without connection. Tamerlane, angry, instructed his soldiers to increase the number to five hundred. On hearing this, Juha burst out laughing, as he thought of the state the poor soldier would be in when the punishment had been inflicted. Tamerlane became utterly furious now, the malice almost popping from his eyes.

"Give him eight hundred lashes," he said.

At this, Juha became almost helpless with laughter. Tamerlane rose.

"You traitor to the prescribed limits!" he cried. "Do you mock the legal limit I decreed—you whose turban is the size of a millstone, knowing yourself in the presence of a mighty man at whose power the whole earth trembles?"

"What you say is correct, Sire," the shaikh answered, "and I realize well enough how weighty this matter is. Yet one thing puzzles me. You are either ignorant of numbers, or else you are different from all us human creatures! How much is eighty lashes, compared to a full eight hundred? It slips off the tongue easily enough. The difficult part is carrying it out. For who can withstand eight hundred lashes?"

❀

When Juha was in Tamerlane's entourage, the despot went on a journey into the provinces, so as to assure himself the multitudes were meek in the face of his tyranny and their subjugation beneath his power.

"On the first day," Juha recounted, "we came to a village where a raging fire had destroyed the buildings and made the people homeless, leaving the place just an empty shell. 'Let the fire destroy them all,' was Tamerlane's response.

"On the second day, we came to a village where, so we were told, a building had fallen in on the inhabitants, leaving large numbers of men, women and children dead under the rubble. The tyrant chuckled. 'Why,' he asked, 'did they let the building cave in to start with?'

"The third day found us in a village where buildings and people alike had been destroyed by a torrential flood sweeping down from the mountain. 'Why,' the tyrant asked, when told about this, 'didn't they divert the flood?'

"On the fourth day, we reached a village where, we were told, a bull had run wild and gone around goring people, slitting some people's bellies and plucking out the eyes of others. The tyrant laughed. 'This brave bull,' he said, 'would be worth a place in my army.'

"I was dismayed"—Juha continued—"at all the disasters and ugly scenes I was seeing. I bowed to the tyrant, pleading and entreating.

"'Our lord Sultan!' I said. 'Propitious omens appear wherever you set foot, and portents of plenty are set in place wherever you make your stay, on every day that dawns on these people—from your Majesty's very approach! If you pursue your journey further, I am afraid the country itself will be destroyed, and your subjects will perish utterly!'"

⁂

When spring came, Tamerlane took Juha along with him to see his soldiers trained in archery. During the practice Tamerlane decided to have some fun with Juha and told him to use a bow and arrow himself, threatening him with the direst punishments if he missed the target. Juha tried to free himself from the trap, but Tamerlane would brook no refusal.

Juha's first arrow missed the target. "That," he said promptly, "is the way our chief of police shoots." His second arrow missed the target too, and he said, "That's the way our city governor shoots."

By sheer luck, his third arrow found the target. "And that," he declared triumphantly, "is the way I shoot." Tamerlane so admired Juha's wit that he presented him with a generous gift.

⁂

The prince of the country (encouraged by the flattery poured out on him by countless people) always claimed he was a poet—indeed the foremost poet in the region. One day, after he'd recited one of his poems, his entourage started heaping praise, striving to point out the wondrous points of rhetoric and the mastery embodied in the poem—all except Juha, who said nothing.

"Didn't you like it?" the prince asked him. "It's a literary masterpiece surely!"

"I don't see any mastery there," Juha answered.

The prince, furious, ordered Juha to be shut up in the stable, and there he stayed for a whole month.

On a later occasion the prince composed another poem and recited it when Juha was present. Juha quickly rose and made to leave, but the prince stopped him.

"Where are you going?" he asked.

"To the stable, my lord prince!" Juha answered.

❧

When Juha was a boy, the governor signed a decree forbidding the carrying of weapons. One day Juha was going to school, and he was caught carrying a long knife and taken in front of the governor.

"Don't you know," the governor told him, "that I've forbidden people to carry weapons? How is it you're carrying this knife, in broad daylight?"

"I'm only carrying it," Juha answered, "to correct mistakes I find in the textbooks."

"Well," the governor said, "surely you can do it without a big knife like that."

"Sir," Juha answered, "some of the mistakes are so huge even this knife isn't big enough for them!"

❧

"Who's more important," Juha was asked one day, "the sultan or the farmer?"

"The farmer, of course," Juha answered. "If he didn't produce any grain, the sultan would starve to death."

Tamerlane took Juha with him to the public bath. After disrobing, and with nothing but a loincloth around his midriff, the tyrant asked:

"How much would you buy me for, if I was offered in the marketplace the way I am now?"

"Fifty dinars," Juha answered.

"What are you saying?" Tamerlane demanded. "Why, the loincloth alone's worth around fifty dinars!"

"That's just the price I had in mind," said Juha.